# BEYOND T ̶ ̶ ̶ ̶IBLE

## FLYING FROM FEAR TO FREEDOM

# GREG HAMERTON

a novel about fresh air

**Other titles by the same author**
The Fresh Air Site Guide
The Riddler's Gift
Second Sight
The Journey

**Beyond the Invisible**
First published November 1998
Reprinted September 1999
New edition January 2007
Paperback and Digital edition June 2011

**Publishers**
ETERNITY PRESS
info@eternitypress.com
www.eternitypress.com

ISBN 978-1-920436-11-7

# DEDICATION

to my friends
　　who help me to fly.

# FOREWORD

The sky offers many things to pilots. In its tumbling crumbling castles of cumulus I find myself challenged, time and time again, as I strive to break through my fears, to grow; to fly!

Fear limits me, it forms an invisible boundary to my life. Within this boundary, the world becomes known, controlled and comfortable. This novel is about pushing through the fears, to discover what lies beyond.

Whatever wonderful craft you fly, be it a paraglider, hangglider, balloon or the armchair of your imagination, I hope that you will join me on a journey into the wild freedom of the sky.

Here impressions and moments of insight are threaded together to capture the esoteric nature of flying. Do I blur the line between fact and fantasy? What matters is what you believe is possible, for this creates much of what you will find when you take your step off the edge of your known world; a step beyond the invisible.

Believe, and you will fly!

*Greg Hamerton*
Cape Town, South Africa,
February 2007

# BREATHLESS

Reach out, leap off, accept the dare!
The exhilaration of suspension in air
swirls in our blood, our minds, in our senses
ecstatically cold as the sunlight drenches
the jagged peaks warm in consummate bliss
and we taste the high cloud's vaporous kiss

Transcend the limits of your imminent scare -
Reach out, leap off, accept the dare!

# BIG SKY LIFE

The wind sighed through the pines above my head. Another
thermal was passing, carrying its rising promise to that special high
place where it would become sky. The air smelled as clean as the
clear stream which gurgled by the path. A squirrel scolded me from
the boughs above. I shouldn't be carrying such a big backpack up the
mountain, it would be the death of me.

"Don't worry, little guy," I said cheerfully, "it's worth it."

It most certainly was. How many hills had I carried my paraglider
up, how many steps had I shared with her, only to be repaid one-
thousand-fold when she carried me? My backpack had become a part
of me, this was the sixth week since leaving town.

There was more time to think, out here, I mused. It was fun, just
drifting from one adventure to another, looking for new places to fly.
What was it that had kept me in the city so long? I couldn't remember.
Another thermal gust brushed the path ahead, swirling the forest
scents about, filling me with excitement.

There had always been some commitments in town, and no matter
how fast I met them, they would be replaced, just as demanding as
before. Go to work, strive, stress, fight, succeed, bring home more
money, but hey! I worked so hard I deserve to enjoy my time off, so

I buy this, and one of those, and some of that, I need to be over there now! I need a faster car, a better cellphone, I want new clothes I want a new image, I'd better rush, there's a meeting at four. There are better things out there for those who work harder, what about the future? You can never tell if there is a big disaster on its way so save up loads of money, stash it away, you need to be safe, back to work, strive, stress, succeed, bring home more money, but hey! I worked so hard I deserve to enjoy my time off.

Outside of that rut the world was scary, unknown, full of risk and uncertainty, offering no security, no escalating financial rewards to match an escalating desire to spend. I had felt the dis-ease, I was sick in spirit, but how could I stop when the city was my only source of sustenance?

It was as easy as pointing my car out of town. And thus the Big Sky Life had begun, or so I called it.

"Twit!twittwit!" a blue-green flash of feathers teased me as it cannon-balled past.

"So I was, but I'm learning now!" I shouted back, but the bird was gone, leaving me alone with my thoughts. A stile straddled the fence ahead, providing a good rest. Standing on the top step I could see the soft grass of the landing field bending in the breeze far below. A shadow appeared in the corner of the field and yes, there it was, peering through the trees I could just make out the fluffy beginnings of a cumulus cloud, the ideal gliding cloud, beckoning to me to come out and play. I scrambled down the stile and up through the bracken.

All days in nature are fantastic, I thought. Sometimes I just lacked the perspective to see it. So many times I had visualised this scene - the fresh air, the sunshine, the excitement of exploring. At last I was living the dream. I crested the hill and strode out through the wildflowers.

This was what I was created for! To be outside, in the wind, breathing in the effervescent scents of spring. I tossed my backpack onto the grass and ran in wide circles under the brilliant blue sky. I chased startled butterflies from bush to bush. Beetles scurried into the undergrowth. With the weight of my backpack removed I felt that I could float away. I leaped through the grasses; an astronaut on the moon. Mad, or sane, I felt alive.

A thermal murmured through the grass. I hurried to prepare my paraglider for a flight. The yellow fabric crinkled loudly as I shook the knots out of the thin suspension lines. The design still amazed me.

Such light fabric, such a simple concept - the cells sewn together in an aerofoil canopy with the pilot's harness far below. There it lay, a triumph for all the dreamers who for centuries believed that one day, it could be done. My eagle-body in a bag.

The glider snagged on a little bush as I pulled her up and I let her fall back gently, playing with the wind. I cleared the lines. It was quiet, even the birds had stopped singing for a moment.

My glider came up smoothly the second time, pulling at the harness, wanting to rise, eager to start the day's adventure.

Wait for the moment, I told myself. There's a perfect time for every beginning, I had to wait until it felt right.

There it was! That butterfly-happy-scared squirm in my stomach, my intuition's eager nudge, so I let my glider go and she flew me skywards.

How beautiful the sky was, up close. The lifting air was smooth. Every day it seemed easier for me to find, amidst the shifting air currents. I turned to the right on reflex, and flew into a thermal pushing its way towards the heavens. And to think that the thermal would have gone to waste if I hadn't been flying that day! How many go wasted every day?

The ground sank further and further away, and the colours of the forests and grasses melted together, swirling into a green pool as I gained altitude. The wind whistled softly through my lines, causing them to hum in tension. And I flew, high over the world, hanging by a thread.

I watched the earth drift slowly by. How beautiful it was! Suspended in the elemental majesty of the wind, even time seemed to loosen its grip and I was alone in the poetry of flight.

In silence.

We had been there forever, it seemed. But after a time, I noticed the thinness of the lines, and sensed the fluttering fragility of the wing above my head. I saw the light carabiners that connected my glider to the harness. I felt gravity yawning up at me. Pulling me down, down to the solid ground that would break me if I fell.

Suddenly the ground was coming up to join me and I was swinging around to make a difficult landing between the gnarled tree and the tumbled rocks and the air was rushing out of my glider in a reluctant hoosh! Gone, the thin cool air of altitude, full of dreams and sights unseen. Having offered me just a taste of freedom, the sky had become even more alluring, by escaping from my grasp.

"I am a better pilot for today," I whispered to my glider.

Better, because I wanted to fly again.

That feeling, that passion is worth a lot. I sometimes wonder if we only live because we want to live. If we lost the passion for it, we would cease to be. Certainly this is true with flying. We fly because we want to fly. It's the desire that makes it possible.

# WILDLIFE!

Later, as the sun was setting in a bronze sky, I set off to find a campsite. I had walked a long way to retrieve my car, after flying so defiantly away from it. I was tired, elated, and very hungry. So I spun my wheels in the gravel and drove off in search of the perfect place.

I turned off the main road and onto a winding track that led into a narrow valley. I could just make out a little lake in the gathering gloom. Beside the lake stood a forest of oaks, subtle shades in the twilight. I love forests, they are always quiet, so secretive and protective. I was looking forward to a cosy night.

My campfire cast a flickering light against the trees. Something good bubbled under the lid of my billycan, escaping in steaming tendrils to flavour the air with herbs. My mind drifted back to my flight - the gentle thermals and clean, clear air.

I was lucky, I reflected, to be out there, so free. There seemed to be more substance to my life in the wilds, more possibilities for growth. I felt as if I was awakening from a long sleep; the sleep of technology, of modernity, of suburbia.

"Pah!" scoffed my billycan as a puff of steam blew the lid off. It was time to eat. I tested the steaming broth and smiled in satisfaction. Hunger really was the best sauce. It was an instant pasta from the supermarket, but it tasted great. I settled down next to the fire and enjoyed the evening meal.

The flames waved and twisted in the coals, creating faces and shapes. The wood crackled. I tossed another log on the fire, and the sparks swirled up into the thickening night.

By the time that I had finished supper, my legs had become numb. Sleep crept upon me. I knew I should douse the fire and pitch the tent and get into my sleeping bag, but I just didn't. have. the energy.

A cold night breeze came down off the hills. I scraped some leaves together for a pillow. I wrapped my jacket around me and settled with a sigh onto the forest floor. I slept for some hours, and the night drew closer.

I was vaguely aware that I was cold. The jacket just couldn't cover enough of my body; there would always be a small patch where the cold would creep up my back. I tried again to pull the jacket further down, but discovered again that it was caught under my body because I was lying on it. There was something digging into my hip. My neck was stiff. I was cold.

Slowly I lifted myself off the squashed leaves. I saw the ashes of the dead fireplace; the fire had burned out. The night chill had crept into everything. The trees loomed out of the forest, blocking the stars. The ground was knurled and bony, making me feel vulnerable and soft. I shivered.

CRACK!

A branch, broken like a gunshot. I looked about in panic, searching for some clue in the darkness. The night pressed in on me, and the trees tilted towards me, from all sides. I couldn't see. I couldn't see!

Surely it couldn't be a leopard, crunching through the forest towards the scent of my campsite? It had to be just a branch, old and weak which had suddenly, for no reason at all, fallen off the tree it was on.

CRACK! CRACK! CRUNCH!

Whatever it was, it was enormous! I was on my feet and running. I fled for the car. Images of slashing claws and wolverine jaws chased me from behind. I was at the car in seconds, and just needed to pull out the keys to unlock the door. But I couldn't find them. I searched my trouser pockets, then my jacket, frantic. At last I found them, in a pocket I was sure I'd checked.

The key jammed in the door.

Oh pleasepleaseplease open you damned thing!

I squinted at the key. It was the wrong one of the bunch. I fumbled for the correct key, my hands shaking.

CRACK! Another branch. CRAAAACKKKK!

By the sounds of it, the beast had just pushed over a whole tree. I ripped the door open and slammed it shut behind me, staring into the dark. I breathed with short gasps and my heartbeat pounded in my ears. I tried to see what was coming out of the forest but a mist had appeared. It took a while to realise the mist was on the inside of the windowpane. I smeared the window dry and peered out into the night.

I didn't want to leave all my cooking gear and food out, but if the beast was big enough to push down trees, then I would high-tail out of there and may the cooking gear rest in peace. I started the car's engine, revved it mercilessly. I turned the headlights on, and swung the car to shine its light into the forest.

Nothing emerged. I couldn't be sure if the branches had stopped snapping; the car was making a lot of noise.

A calm voice sounded in my head.

*Not much of a hero, are you?*

"I didn't say that I was."

*What about stepping into the unknown, releasing your fears, releasing the need for security, for safety?*

"But this is different! There is a great big creature out there in the dark, pushing trees over!"

*Observe your body.*

"My body?"

*Just observe it.*

"My body's fine, I'm not hurt. Well, it is all tensed up, my muscles are knotted, my heartbeat's too fast, my breathing is shallow, but I am ready to run when that beast comes for me."

*Yet you haven't seen anything. Nothing has come out of the forest. What is it?*

"I don't know what it is!"

*Ahh, the Unknown.*

"The Unknown?" I paused. My inner voice was playing a game of analogy with me. It led me to thinking. Was the forest somewhat like the world of adventure I had stepped into? And that my fear of the hidden beast was somehow the same as my fear of any unknown thing which might challenge me. I'd already conquered my need for security, I'd left the city life behind, but here I was, clinging to safety once again.

I glanced into the night. Surely the beast was about to tear out of the forest toward me?

*Your mind is as tense as your body. How long do you think you can live like this for? How well do you think your mind operates when clenched in fear? You'll soon tire, and think feebly.*

"I still don't see the parallel," I challenged my inner voice.

*How long did part of your mind stay clenched in fear in the city? Fear of losing security, fear of losing comfort?*

"Well, forever, it seems."

*And you felt alive only when you released these fears?*

I was beginning to understand.

I was in the Unknown, the forest. I had heard a noise, I had reacted in fear, and allowed my mind to create substance for the fear. I had run for my old security, the car. And so I had lost a chance to live fearlessly, and had become my Old Self once again. Locked up, fearful, safe.

"But there's a big animal out there!"

*Is there?*

The only fact was that there had been a noise. The rest was unknown.

*So step out the car and live confidently, urged my inner voice. Explore reality, don't make it up in your imagination.*

"But what if it really is a big animal?"

*What if it isn't?*

"I will still be safe in the car, either way."

*Safe. But smaller, somehow. Less.*

The beast had still not shown its head. The car purred along, having warmed up to a constant idling speed.

Eventually I summoned up the courage to get out of the car. The cold air rushed to meet me as I poked my head out of the door. I stepped gingerly onto the ground, not wanting to make too much noise, lest I be spotted. I kept my hand on the car door.

CLUNK! CLATTER!

I was back in the car, my face glued to the window. The beast! It had made a sound from the campsite. A beast that could knock down trees! I was shivering again, but I was overcome with a morbid fascination. I wanted to see what it was that I feared.

But to do so I had to first put aside the fear itself, and leave the car.

I spent the night creating a face for my fear, imagining what it could be, giving it flesh, giving it menace, giving it power.

Some hours later the sky began to lighten from the east, an agonising, gradual shift of paler shades that never released the forest from its gloom until the sun finally pierced the horizon.

The daylight dissolved the creatures of my vivid imagination. Had I really heard such loud sounds? I cracked my door open, and eased myself out on stiff legs. There was dew on the grass. There was a forest with some trees.

Clunk! Clank!

My billycan. In the rocks beside the path. It was moving.

Kedunk! It fell over onto its side. It wriggled. Then it rolled back onto the path and revealed a furry tail, and a grey-brown body. The small creature chased the billycan and butted it. Then it stopped as it made eye contact with me and stood on its hind legs in surprise.

A meerkat, a burrowing creature related to a mongoose. Height: maybe 50 cm on his hind legs. A shy scavenger. Special skills: preys on snakes.

The meerkat was probably developing its own definition. A human. Big clumsy hairless thing with funny smell. Too slow to catch me. Watching me. His food, maybe?

Thanks for the supper, the meerkat seemed to say, before it scampered into the grass. I watched where it had gone. A twig snapped as it passed through the bushes, then all was quiet.

Surely the little meerkat was too small to snap the branches I had heard breaking in the night? There had to be tracks in the forest of the real beast, the great hairy tree-rending ogre. I was fighting to justify my night of fear, but I was losing ground against the advance of reason.

The campfire was untouched, a grey circle on the forest floor. I could see the imprint of my body in the leaves beside it. A packet of cereal lay scattered over my cooking gear. A nibble had been taken out of the bread. Everything else was in its place. No swathe of destruction, no vicious gouges in the ground, no flattened cooker or exploded boxes. I began to search further from the campsite, wandering into the woods.

All I could find was an old tree, a collapsed jumble of rotten limbs some distance away from the campsite. The broken trunk suggested it had fallen in on its own weight. I blew the dust of fine wood splinters into the air. It smelt old, dry.

I cursed under my breath as I tested one of the branches. It was rotten to the core and fell away without resistance.

CRACK!

I walked slowly back to the campsite; my stiffness easing, my doubts fading away.

"Oh if someone had been watching this," I hooted to myself, "how they would have cried with laughter!"

*Oh but I am watching you*, my inner voice answered.

We laughed for some time, myself and I, as the colours and scents of the new day gathered and the sun climbed in a brilliant blue sky. I have had many teachers in my life, but none so memorable as the knee-high meerkat.

I went flying again. It was flyable that day and the next, soft flying with gentle winds. I travelled slowly east, moving on every evening to a new town, meeting new people. By the end of a week I had reached the towering Drakensberg Mountains. The flying would be dangerous amongst the dramatic cliffs and steep-sided valleys. I knew my ability to transcend my fears would be tested here more than ever.

# EAGLEFRIEND

A chain ladder clung to the rockface above me, pinned into the cliff with bolts of steel. Its metal rungs were age-worn with the passage of climbers who had passed before me. A signboard stated that nobody was taking responsibility for me climbing up the ladder but myself. Seemed pretty reasonable, I thought, considering the way the ladder swung between its pins. Nobody likes to be responsible for crazy people.

An icy wind was shrieking down from the peaks, sucking the warmth from my clothes, chilling me to the marrow. This was the west-wind, known to be extremely hazardous for flying in the Drakensberg. The west-wind tumbled down through the teeth of the rocky escarpment and emerged twisted and angry. It would blow strongly, full of turbulence, flowing for miles over the plains before finding relative calm.

On my back I carried my paraglider. For better or for worse, I was going to carry my glider up to the peaks, to attempt a flight.

I knew I couldn't fly in this. It was madness. It was too windy.

But I was living the Big Sky Life, and my paraglider went everywhere with me, partly for the challenge and partly just in case. I had learned my lesson about judging things. You can never tell when it might just become flyable. I tightened my straps and began the ascent of the exposed ladder. The cold peaks crowded in above me, vertiginous and beautiful.

The wind toyed with the ladder, pushing me off-balance. The chain-links clanked dully against the rock, a musical sound like some ancient mantra drawn from the rocks' memory and released into the theatre of this tall retreat. I glanced back, taking in the fall of the land, the raw carve of the ancient river-courses that scribed deep lines of care upon the mountain. Far below me, the rivers joined in a pale blue lake. The water surface was swirling with restless catspaws.

It was slow going up the ladder. I could only progress once I had balanced on every rung. The backpack was unsteady in the gale. I clutched at the ladder with both hands.

During the ascent I stayed warm from the exercise, but when I emerged on the plateau, the full blast of the west-wind hit me. It was exposed and flat, and bitterly cold. I donned my flying suit and helmet, then strode off to find shelter amongst the cliffs. The paths veered off in all directions through the scrawny vegetation.

So many pathways in life, each splitting at a choice, I mused. One must choose wisely, lest the wrong path was followed. Strangely enough they all seemed to lead across the plateau to the cliffs, some just spent more time detouring through the scrub.

The edge of the plateau was dramatic. The cold west-wind gusted at my back, threatening to push me off the cliffs. Deep valleys ran out into the lowlands like folds in an emerald green garment. Lush vegetation crowded into the river-courses and spilled onto the slopes. Trees thrived in the shelter of the mountains. Below me there were amphitheatres filled with waving grasses. Empty foothills, resplendent in their simplicity, curved and twisted idly at the mountain's feet. There were no signs of habitation, no signs of mankind.

I absorbed the simple beauty of nature.

I discovered a narrow ledge jutting out from the cliff-face and clambered down to it. The wind howled above my head where I sat protected by the cliff. The sunlight pushed weakly against me, thawing my bones. I leant back against my paraglider, waiting for the weather to change. Time passed slowly.

The exposure had stimulated my perception; the landscape stood out in sharp focus. I could see far out across the plains to the horizon, where a bank of cloud was sliding over the land. From my elevated perspective I could see the top of the cloudbank, a majestic carpet of white on an underfelt of shadows. It curled and swirled like whipped cream. The sun picked out the biggest wisps, and they became radiant translucent angels.

It is probably like this every day out here, I thought, every new day offered new beauty, new colours and natural forms, deeply satisfying patterns of earth, air, water and life.

I wondered what the beauty was, what was its essential nature, that it could make me smile and leave my soul so enraptured? It was a mystery. And although I had been out for hikes before, but hadn't experienced the beauty so tangibly before. Something had changed in my world.

Maybe my old life of security and comfort was like a small building. My world had been contained by my fears, and all I had known and perceived was the fortress. By accepting the risks of adventure I had gone beyond the fortress walls, and as I walked further into the Unknown so I grew, in spirit and in sense, perceiving more of the reality that had been there all along.

If only someone had shown me this before, I wouldn't have wasted so much time, going in circles. If only someone would show me the way forward, I would walk the road to mastery. I sensed that there was a lot more I was capable of than merely sensing beauty. But where to begin?

I gazed down the depths of the cliffs which fell beneath me. The rock curved back underneath itself, forming a concave face. The drop called out to me with a strange allure.

A rock clattered past me from above. It hit the ledge hard, spinning out into the space created by the concave cliffs, tumbling over and over, falling and growing smaller until it had disappeared. Then another one was skittering down toward me. I leapt to my feet. Was something moving up there? There was nothing obvious.

My eye caught the movement just in time, and I ducked. I heard the whip of broken air as another stone raced past me. What was up there? An animal moving just out of sight? Was the rockface about to shift and slip off the cliff, tumbling me and my thoughts into the abyss?

My mouth was dry. I had the feeling that someone was watching me. My blood boiled. Was it a herd-boy, throwing stones? I had to get moving.

Then a boulder sailed off the cliff and crashed onto a ledge close by. Although it had missed me, my legs grew weak as I saw a sizeable portion of ledge tear away and thunder over the abyss. A boulder? It was too big to have been thrown. This cliff was collapsing.

I wanted to climb, but there was my paraglider. I groaned. I couldn't leave my wing behind. I needed it. Without a wing, I was just a wanderer. I hoisted it onto my back, then scrambled up the rocky slope. The weight of my paraglider pushed me off-balance. I fell, tipping towards the impending drop. The rock bit into my knees.

I shouted at myself in frustration and lurched to my feet again. I should have left the paraglider behind. It would be too ironic if I died because I carried my folded wings on my back.

*And so you stumble to meet the Unknown with your baggage,* prompted my inner voice. *The paraglider is your identity. Why do you cling to it so?*

"Not now!" I yelled. Why did my inner voice insist on being the philosopher at moments like these?

*All right, if you want to crawl on the surface of reality, so be it.*

I shimmied up the sheer slope. If this chunk of rock went, I was going to slide off in a tremendous roaring wall of death. My chest burned as I forced my legs to pump faster. Blood flowed from my damaged knees, but I could not feel anything. My body was flooded with adrenaline. Yet the rocks had stopped falling, I noticed. It was rather quiet, besides my gasping and groaning.

I burst over the crest of the cliff like a wild man, with a heaving chest and the apocalypse in my eyes. I ran straight into him, I didn't even see he was there until it was too late.

He was a tall man. The way he held his body suggested an agility that matched his strength. His muscles were iron-hard from exercise, his face was tanned. His mat of black hair whipped in the wind. His shoulders shook with laughter.

I looked straight into his grey eyes. I was confused for a moment. I hadn't expected laughter. The stranger looked at me and I saw a flicker of decision cross his face. Then he lunged forwards, thrusting me away from him. I reeled backwards toward the edge of the cliff.

"What are you doing? Are you crazy!" I shouted in a panic-stricken squeak.

He grinned. His eyes twinkled with a secret knowledge. I tried to turn to the side, to avoid his advance, but he caught my arm in an iron grip and twisted me sharply back towards him, my back to the fall. He stepped in close, pushed me off-balance, and grabbed hold of my other flailing arm.

He had me on the edge. I couldn't breathe. My feet were on the last rock that jutted over the cliffs. I teetered over the precipice, my backpack pulling me from behind, threatening to drag me over. I tried to pull myself forward on his arms, but he grinned even wider than before and pushed me out a little further.

"What are you doing?" I asked, in a deathly whisper.

"Buying myself time," he responded in a confident voice.

Time? I struggled to think through the fear. How would killing me buy him time?

"Why do you want to kill me?" I asked.

He shook his head, laughing as he did so.

"You aren't going to kill me? Then what are you doing?"

"Buying myself time," he answered. His incessant grin was beginning to irritate me. Why did he have to be so cryptic? What was he doing up here anyway? Then I understood. He was the culprit.

"Were you throwing rocks at me?" I bellowed. "You were throwing rocks at me! What right do you have? You could have bloody killed me, you idiot!"

His grin faded. He released his grip. That made me shut up very quickly.

Clinging on to his arms with my heart hammering, I searched his face for answers. He gazed back at me, and grinned again. He kept his arms extended towards me, allowing me to hold on, but he did not re-grip my arms. It looked as if he were prepared to stand there pushing me out over the cliff for a long, long time. The wind howled around us, drawing the heat of my anger out of me.

I became more lucid. The more I looked at it, the more I realised that anger wouldn't serve me. My fury would be more dangerous than the falling rocks, for the trickster, on whose arms I hung, held all the trump cards. Me, in particular.

His gaze never left my face, he seemed to read my expression. Yet he wasn't hostile. A pendant hung from his neck, an intriguing structure of interlocking black and white wood engaged in a battle for supremacy. He was dressed in an old fashion, with a rough, black tunic belted with white cord at the waist, tan coloured trousers, leather boots. His skin was weathered. He watched me, patiently, like a teacher waiting kindly for a slow student.

I finally broke the silence. "What am I missing?"

"You haven't thought about the eagles," he offered.

I was too drained to argue with him. I just wanted to understand.

"What have eagles got to do with it?"

"When you are in the mountains, you should always consider the eagle's perspective. What will it think of you?"

I looked up, down, around.

"What eagle?" I asked, mystified.

"The eagle that had just killed a mouse and was flying back to her nest. The nest you were sitting above. She would have attacked you to protect her chicks."

I hadn't seen any nest, but the cliff had been concave beneath me.

"She had two chicks in that nest and eagles are fiercely protective. You would have had more than just a bloody knee," he said.

"How did you know?"

"I have been here since sunrise," he replied.

Sunrise! But that would have meant that he had walked up during the night. In the storm.

"Come off it! You couldn't have been here that long. I didn't see you when I came up here."

"You don't see very well," he replied. "You need to use the eagle's perspective."

I glared up at him. But I had to accept that maybe he was right.

"Why didn't you just shout to me to climb up. Why the rocks?"

"Much more fun, don't you think?" He laughed at my feigned anger. He knew I had lost my rage, I was scared and cold.

"More fun to make me run in fear from a rockslide, to bloody my knees, and to push me out over the cliff?" I asked, incredulous.

But the fear and the bloody knees were of my own making. As was the need for him to immobilise me on the cliff edge, to let me cool off. Things could have been different if I'd responded with less fear. Instead I'd built my own personal monster, visualising an avalanche.

"All I did was throw a few rocks in warning." He grinned. "Well, there was one big rock, but I threw that one quite wide. It wouldn't be right, to endanger the eagles." He laughed at my expression again, rocking on his heels and gripping my arms once again to steady himself. "There's nothing so powerful as personal monsters."

It felt as if he had picked that thought out of my mind.

I might have felt uneasy, but his laughter was infectious. He seemed so sure of himself, so vibrant and full of life. In contrast I felt small, as if I had let myself down by panicking, and by losing the control of my anger. I remembered having felt like this before, in the forest, after the night with the billycan. So I hadn't learned that lesson yet, and understanding how my fear created reality didn't mean I wouldn't face fear again.

Next time, I'd be ready.

"Fears are sheep in wolves clothing," he stated, as if it was the definitive answer to all my questions. Again, there was that wierd sense that he'd responded to something I'd thought, and not said.

"Baa-aa." I answered.

He laughed, and pulled me from the edge of the cliff. I was flooded with relief.

His name was Bartholomew, but most people called him Eaglefriend, or Beagle for short. He was a member of The Eagle Protectorate, working for the World Wildlife Federation, roaming the mountain parks and studying 'everything with a beak and talons'. It took a while for me to learn this from him as we walked. He turned my questions upside down, answered in mysteries, and disappeared in mid-conversation to inspect signs of eagles (where all I could see were scattered bones). I told him more about myself in the process of questioning him than I had expected. By the time we had descended to the shelter of the Mountain Club hut I had almost told him my life's story.

And all the while he nodded sagely, as if he knew the story already, as if he recognised who I was or where I was.

The hut was a rough stone-and-cement building, capped with corrugated iron roofing. It hunkered down on the mountain slope fully exposed to the wind. Inside, it was gloomy. There was just a stove and three bunkbeds, and a steel water bucket, dented from age and use, graffiti scratched into the metal. I took it outside to find some water. A wire fence ran across the mountain just beyond the hut, marking the end of the reserve, but the world on the far side of that fence looked equally wild and remote. There was a stream nearby, with ice-cold water.

As if by magic, Beagle produced provisions from a backpack under the bunks. He hadn't been carrying the bag, and he hadn't been in the hut the night before; I had been there alone. There was something altogether strange about him.

But he was a good cook, and we were soon savouring a hot meal. The fire burned down in the stove and hissed quietly to itself, filling the bare room with a mellow warmth and the smell of wood-smoke. It was dark and cold outside the window, where the moon soon cast her spell over the peaks and washed the landscape in silver.

Beagle began to play a melody on his flute, and I settled into my sleeping-bag on the bunkbed and listened. The wind whistled over the roof, a mournful accompaniment. From time to time a gust sneaked in under the eaves and I would feel a cold breath on my neck. Beagle's tune was intriguing, a high pattern worked around a simple low refrain.

It was enchanting. The candle that was stuck to the bedpost threw a flickering light on his face. The melody rose and fell, pulling me away with the music, dreaming of flying. I hummed along for a while, and I made up a poem to go with the music.

> *Now and then you'll hear the tale*
> *of pilots young and old*
> *who push too far against the gale,*
> *fly too high and bold.*
> *They're all gone, for in their heart*
> *they didn't learn the lore*
> *it is rare and risky art*
> *to leave the earth and soar.*

My mind drifted, and I followed a new verse as it came to me. It was fun, making it up as I went along, and yet the words came to me as if I'd heard them before, as if I was just remembering them. But it's often like that, with creating poems. They seem to come from somewhere else. I whispered along, following the story.

> *And once there was a cheeky crow*
> *who boldly braved the storms,*
> *he flew up through the swirling snow*
> *to ice and sparks and fearsome forms.*
> *Thunderbolts crashed to the ground*
> *and ripped against his side,*
> *the air grew dark and full of sound,*
> *it ate him up, and so he died.*

> *When he reached the other place*
> *where spirits find their rest*
> *the crow found nothing there to face*
> *there was no final test.*
> *There was just a choice to take*
> *to come back to the sky*
> *choose to live and live and live again*
> *or die and die and die.*

*The crow fell as a lightning strike*
*then spread his wings out wide*
*and he thought that it was good to fly*
*and so began to glide.*
*He moved away across the land*
*and cried out as he flew,*
*"Hark! Hark! Hark!" he sang with glee*
*and lived his life anew.*

*So praise the crow, who changed his mind*
*and tells us of the storm.*
*Praise the crow and all their kind*
*who take the wingéd form.*

Beagle finished his tune on a long note, which drifted with my thoughts into the night sky. He smiled at me and nodded, as if he had taken part in my singing and had enjoyed it too. Had I sung it out loud? I couldn't be sure.

# THE EAGLE'S PERSPECTIVE

The next day dawned grey and foul. The wind had increased, bringing with it a rolling mass of grey cloud that poured down from the peaks. The cloud rushed past the hut, dampening the window with driven moisture.

Beagle was gone. His pack had disappeared from under the bed. He had left without so much as a goodbye! I eased off the bunkbed onto the floor. Jeepers! it was cold. The fire needed stoking. I hurriedly pulled on my socks and hiking boots. I paused once I had opened the door. The soggy vegetation was being blown around in the gale. It would be hard to find dry firewood in this weather.

Something thudded to the floor behind me. I spun in surprise. Beagle pushed me on the chest. I stumbled backwards, off balance. My foot clipped the doorjamb, and I fell out of the hut. Beagle was hooting with laughter as I tumbled onto the soggy pathway.

"Always be prepared!" Beagle shouted gleefully and slammed the door. I could hear the door being barred, from inside.

Damn! He was a boisterous fellow. How had I missed him in the hut? It was a five-metre-square stone construction with nothing in it.

"Okay, okay, very clever!" I shouted at him through the closed door. "Where were you hiding?"

"You don't see very well. You need to learn the eagle's perspective." As if it was some unique method of vision, like a third eye stuck in your forehead, or something.

"Let me in, it's awful out here!" I heaved on the door, but it was firmly closed.

"No, you'll need to find another way in," taunted Beagle.

I wasn't going to plead with him, I was going to get even. I slipped around the side of the hut to see if there were any other possible entrances besides the front door. Maybe a loose roofsheet, or the back window.

There was nothing. The hut was very simple. There was only one entrance - the door. I decided on another tactic. There was a boulder on the one side of the hut where I could hide. If Beagle wouldn't let me in, I would pretend to leave and wait until he came out. From where I sat he would not see me as he opened the door. Then I would catch him. I selected out a thick piece of wood to beat him with. I'd show him boisterous, all right. Always be prepared, indeed!

"Fine, I'll find my own shelter!" I shouted to him, and went to hide behind the boulder.

Nothing happened. I grew colder and colder, clutching my cudgel stiffly in shivering hands. My T-shirt grew wet and stuck to my back. The longer I waited, the more chance I had of catching him off guard, because he would not expect me to have been poised for so long. I would not give in. I would prove that I had more patience.

But there was only so much of silence and wind that I could take. Finally I straightened stiffly and tiptoed to the door. The hut was silent. I knocked tentatively on the door with my cudgel. Then loudly. There was no response.

"Okay Beagle, I give up, I've had enough now. Let me in." Was this another one of his lessons in humility? I could be humble, I was frozen. But just let him wait until I'd warmed up again ...

I leaned across the window and peered in. I could not see all of the interior through the water droplets running down the glass, but it appeared empty. One could never be too sure. I tried the door and this time it swung inwards, without resistance.

I rushed through the door to confuse his attack.

The hut was empty. There was no trace of Beagle, not under the bunks, not behind the door, or hanging from the roof. I was confused, but one thing was clear. Beagle had not been in the hut all the time I had been outside on the rock, I would have seen him leave. Which meant that he must have somehow seen me walking around the hut initially and he had sneaked away before I had completed my inspection and returned to the door. I had been sitting in the cold for nothing.

I shouted in frustration, but soon afterwards, I couldn't help laughing at myself. He had me well beaten. I stuffed the cudgel into the stove and added some wood chips I found on the floor. Warmth was more important than weaponry.

Beagle returned in the afternoon, bedraggled and grinning. He didn't say a word; he busied himself at once with cooking up a pot of coffee. He waved a bashed old enamel cup in my direction and I accepted, watching him fill it to the brim with the steaming dark liquid.

He was a strange fellow, but I liked him very much.

"The eagle's perspective?" I asked, at last. I would not ask him how he tricked me, that would just reveal what an idiot I'd been.

"Ah yes, that." He shot me a glance from under his eyebrows. "You spent a long time out there in the wind with that cudgel. Good job you burned it before you could use it on me."

I flushed with embarassment. I had intended to thump him with that stick, no doubt about it.

"How did you see that! I didn't see you watching me."

"Just because I'm far away doesn't mean I can't watch you."

I looked blank.

"Something I learned from the eagles," Beagle explained, "is that vision and sight are separable functions. Sight is a physical process, it's the stimulation in your eyes. Light falls on the retina, chemical processes transmit this to your brain. Vision, on the other hand, involves the mind, it involves imagination and visualisation and the projection of consciousness. Yes, the eagles have very sharp eyesight, but it's what they do with their vision that makes them so special. When you learn to move your attention away from your body, out and upwards, your vision can take in a bigger area than what you can see. I watched you from within the hut. Later I watched you from afar."

I didn't see.

"But what is the difference between sight and vision? How can you see something without physically seeing it?"

"How many objects are on the bed behind you?" he asked. "Don't turn around, just tell me."

I tried to remember what I had seen before I had come across for the coffee. There had been my wet t-shirt, my book. My penknife. I struggled to remember, scanning a picture of the bed held in my mind. A packet of granola bars was there as well.

"Four, I think."

"Good." He smiled. "But there are six," he said, without glancing at the bed behind me. I turned and saw my towel and a pen lying on the bed as well.

"What's that got to do with vision?"

"Well, you made a start there using your memory. That is the beginning of vision. You use the image held in the mind's eye instead of the light coming in through your eyes. But you didn't allow your attention to move from where you were sitting. Try this. The image of the bed you have in your mind, allow your vision to move over it, around it, under it. Slowly you will develop the ability to move out of your memory and into reality."

"But surely that's just imagination?" I objected.

"Imagination helps to create new forms," Beagle answered. "Vision observes real objects in real space. The granola bars have a pricetag of 3-49 on them."

I turned around and checked. He was right. I used the pen and altered the price to 8-49, because I didn't want him to be right. His abilities were fascinating, but also unsettling.

I demanded that Beagle teach me, but he refused. "I've already demonstrated it to you. Teach yourself. You have to figure it out if you want it to work properly. I have some notes to make."

He retreated to the corner of the hut, and there he sat, scribbling in a tattered black book. On the spine was written simply 'Eagles'. He wrote furiously for a while, as if he had discovered something of importance this morning out in the grey, damp gale. I left him alone to his study.

The hut was cold. I sat cross-legged on the floor and experimented with my 'vision'. The concept was wonderful. I would be able to see anywhere! What would it mean for flying? I'd be able to see gusts of wind in bushes far below, and could use that knowledge to guess where the thermals were. I'd be able to fly through clouds, without losing my way. Maybe it really was how eagles hunted, with a movable point of perception. If they could project their awareness down to the ground, they would find their prey so easily. While they cruised high above the earth, they could use their vision to be down on the ground. And when the mouse scuttled out from the ground-cover, the eagle would be aware of it.

I imagined what it would be like to be an eagle, diving down, the wind shrieking over my feathers as I fell towards the mouse, and yet all the time seeing the mouse in sharp focus of my vision. There'd be a glorious moment of impact, talons and speed.

I caught myself dreaming. I tried to see around the room as Beagle had, just sitting on the floor, closing my eyes and thinking myself to the different objects. It seemed pointless all of a sudden, for I was merely sifting through my inaccurate memories of the objects at hand - nothing but a blur filled my mind when I tried to 'see' the top of the coffee pot, a smudge of brown was Beagle's backpack under the bed.

I spread a book out on the bed and sat down with my back to it, attempting to read the open page. It was a complete failure. I had a mental picture of the book with its open page as I had dropped it on the bed. But the page remained a blur of white and black. Really, what had I been expecting? I couldn't transform myself magically into an amazing psychic simply because I wanted to. I grew impatient. Maybe Beagle had used some trick this morning, maybe this theory of vision was just some far-fetched idea to inflate Beagle's mystical image. What was he doing up here anyway? Maybe he was just a fraud, trying to take me for a ride.

He paused from his writing.

"Believe!" he commanded. The word vibrated in the air like a potent spell.

He withdrew again, absorbed in recording his eagle lore.

I understood. To break through, to explore this realm of vision I had to let go of my doubts. Doubt was just like fear, limiting the world to a small fortress of safety, of the Known. If I believed it was possible to move my awareness out of my body, to 'see' things beyond the limits of my sight, then I was stepping into a world where it could be true. If I doubted, it could never be true, for me.

Seeing *is* believing then, I realised.

I walked over to the window. The grey cloud swirled against the glass pane. I love watching an elemental force at play; watching waves build and crash on a rocky coast, or the flickering flames of a logfire. I could spend hours being carried upon the patterns, becoming the patterns, leaving my body behind as I played, being drawn into the experience. I allowed my awareness to drift, to become free.

Go on, take yourself through the cloud, I told myself. I watched the air-currents pour over the rocks, feeling myself twist and tumble. My imagination drew me up the slopes, into the mystery of the rolling clouds. As I lingered there, things became more real. I could see bushes thrashing wetly in the wind, the leaves whipping. Rocks emerged from the mists as I passed them. The slope became steeper, slabs of cliff-rock glistened wetly in the dull light. I angled upwards, toward the peaks. A few rock-rabbits huddled in a shallow cave. They didn't notice me. I swept upwards, against the gale. The cliff became sheer, and I began to feel vertigo.

What if I fell from that height?

A silly fear; I knew I was imagining the ascent, I wasn't actually out there over the wet cliffs. My awareness began to slip back to a the mountain hut where I stood and the cold metal windowframe that was pressed against my face.

With a jolt I caught myself. I had almost lost the experience of vision that was developing. A fear had diverted my attention for just a second, and my perception had begun to narrow. I let go of doubt and fear and smallness, and rejoined my awareness amongst the clouds.

I emerged over the peaks, where the boulders hunched in the gloom and drizzle. Tufts of hardy grass whipped in the wind.

And the weatherman would like to report that it is 50 knots North-Westerly, with cloud on the mountain. I launched my awareness higher, lifting away from the peaks, through the clouds. The featureless moisture flowed past me. Then light filtered through the grey.

I burst out through the crest of the cloudbank into the sunshine. The light dazzled me. It reflected off the cloud below me in an incandescent sea, like sparkling pearls. The cloud formed a smooth curve as it flowed over the peaks and dropped into the valleys beyond. It was perfect and breathtaking in its proportion - it stretched away far along the escarpment, a giant cloth draped over the rumpled table of the Gods.

I felt light and free. I had not realised how depressing the grey murk and relentless wind had been until I was liberated from it. Life seemed so good, from my new perspective. I could see forever. The cloud poured off the escarpment beneath me, and the land extended from beneath the cloud in greens and muted browns, all the way to the distant crisp horizon. The sky above was blue and clear. The sense of space was liberating, the view unlimited.

There was a strange crackling sound. It made me nervous. Sky shouldn't crackle. The sound came towards me, until it was almost in my ears, yet I couldn't identify the source.

Suddenly my awareness shifted, and there was Beagle in front of me. He held a sheet of paper between us. Yet in the paper I still saw the vista of sky and cloud, the view from above the peaks. I struggled to make sense of it, these two images conflicting for my attention. Then Beagle crackled the paper again, and it became more real. My vision of the beautiful sunshine, the clouds and the land, stuttered and was gone. I stared at the words on the page.

*Do you see?*

I missed the beautiful clouds above the mountain peaks. Where was the sun? Why was I in the hut? I wanted to be out there again, soaring in the clear sky above a sparkling tablecloth of cloud. I had been up there, up high and free, my body moving like a bird.

But I'd really been standing in the hut all along, against the chill windowpane, staring into the gale, my eyes unseeing, my mind entranced. For how long? I had lost my sense of time. Five minutes, maybe ten? What I had seen! The light, the cloud and sky!

"The sun is always shining, up there," he commented.

He handed me the note, and I took it, puzzled. The sun is always shining? I hadn't told him anything about my vision. How did he know where I'd been?

"Keep that, to remember the gift you have. It's easy to forget."

"How did you - " I began.

"Vision can be shared," he answered. "You dream quite loudly too. That girl with the dark hair, last night. Man!"

There was a glimmer in his eye. Then he threw back his head and laughed. Now he was fooling with me. I hadn't dreamed about any girls last night. He couldn't see into my dreams. Could he?

\* \* \*

We passed the time that afternoon playing cards.

"You going to be here for much longer?" I asked.

"Depends on the eagles, really. I stay as long as they let me."

"What happens when they don't want you around?"

I had three queens in my hand, and I was feeling confident.

"They stop talking to me."

The eagles spoke to him.

"They talk in *English*?" I asked, not a little mocking.

He gave me a warning look. "Not English, no. They have clear thoughts, and a piercing way of passing them on to their kind. I .. apprehend what they say, and then respond."

I looked at my cards. This guy was serious.

I knew that some kinds of telepathy were possible. When the phone rang at home I sometimes knew who it was before they spoke. But direct mental communication, idea for idea?

"What do they talk about?" I asked.

"Perfection. Grace. They are very much like warriors. An eagle's whole life is about mastery." Beagle pulled a new card from the deck, discarding a queen.

"Did you know the strongest chick kills his sibling in the nest? It's the first act he has to commit. Killing his kin. You start your life like that, and you'll turn out different. They study the art of the killing stroke, they find transcendence when it is perfected. They see things differently. I have learned a lot from them."

I snapped up the queen. Now all I needed was two cards to build a sequence, and I could win. At least I was leading the cards.

"I always thought eagles were hard creatures. I would expect them to be secretive. How do you get them to accept you?"

"I present no resistance, so they do not see me as an adversary. They don't have secrets from each other, they can't. Especially when they are bonded." He smiled and picked up the five of clubs that I had discarded, rejecting another card from his hand.

"I sort of .. sit in .. while they share ideas."

"You spy on them?"

"I'm welcomed, but they don't extend their welcome for long. You see, their thought processes are far more focused than ours. We can try to concentrate on one train of thought, but there is always a chatter of other thoughts in the background of our minds." Just one more card, and I'd have him. A seven or four of spades would do the trick. "While you think of the game at hand, there is another thought waiting to see what your next card is, another thought is anticipating winning if you have a good hand, another thought is wondering how good my hand is. You play the game, but your mind is thinking of the wind and the stars outside, whether it shall be flyable tomorrow, and where these playing cards were made, not so?" He waved his cards in my direction.

"But that allows us to do many things at once," I commented. "It's impossible to think of only one thing."

"You can meditate and calm the mind. We can be more focused, but the eagles are way better. They have commanding thoughts, surrounded by silence."

"So they reject you because you're a chatterbox?"

"Yes, exactly. My thoughts disturb the purity of their contemplation."

Beagle discarded the seven of spades. I had a complete hand now, I could simply pick up the card and win. Beagle placed his cards on the table. A run and four of a kind. He was out.

He grinned like a wolf.

"Funnily enough, it's harder to read a human mind. An eagle's thought, when projected, is as sharp as blade. But we have so much going on all at once in our heads that when we project a thought, a whole tangle of them come across. Communicating becomes impossible."

"Then how do you reach the eagles?" I asked.

"I struggle. Often we have misunderstandings. I have trained myself to focus my thoughts as best I can. Single eagles tolerate the noise out of curiosity, but when they bond with a partner I am usually excluded, at the very moment that I want to be included. That's when their spirits really begin to fly."

He bent forward to gather the cards. His pendant swung idly on its cord. It looked like a twisted root, an interlocking structure of black and white. The flickering candlelight played on his face. His eyes were dark pools; wisdom swirled in their depths. He had spoken of another world, a realm of thought I had never considered before.

He chuckled. "But we must never forget how to play! Another hand?" He dealt without waiting for my answer. I had the feeling that I was going to lose every round of cards. It shouldn't be possible to look into someone else's head.

I tried to concentrate on guarding my thoughts. But what do you think about when you are trying not to think about the things you aren't supposed to think about?

Was he really moving through my mind, or was he just having me on? The whole idea challenged my beliefs, but I knew that if I argued for my old world I would only strengthen my limitations. If I wanted to learn and grow, I had to leave the doubts behind.

# THE SINK MONSTER

The snap of the wind in my wing passed through my body. I lunged against my chest-strap, using my weight to control the eager glider. The breathless moment came, and I was pulled off the slope and into the air.

I have done this a thousand times, but I am always excited by that transition, passing from earth to sky. One moment I am standing on the ground, poised with my wing - the next I am airborne, flying through the vapours, with unlimited adventures lying beyond each carving thermal ride. In that instant of lift-off, I truly come alive.

And yet the most unexpected thing happens - I continue to feel gravity. In all my childhood dreams of flying, I was weightless. But in reality, I feel the taughtness of my lines, I feel my weight, and the harness supporting me. It's the ground that seems to move. It falls away under the pull of some magical force. And I stay where I was, at the centre of the universe, as the earth and the rocks and trees, rivers, valleys, roads, fields of green, fall away from me.

And then I am alone, high in the sky.

The earth spun in wide circles beneath me. I held my wing banked over hard, holding on to a narrow, wild thermal. It was racing upwards, lifting my wing and pushing me outwards into the sinking surrounding air. I banked harder to resist the glider's tendancy to pull out and level off. The rowdy little air-current was going someplace high, and I intended to go with it.

The earth continued to spin below me, creating a kaleidoscope of greens and browns, the rocks, the cliffs, the tumbling waterfall, the hills, the plains, the dusty fields, then the hills and the rocks, the cliffs, the tumbling waterfall once more. I soaked up the joy of the swirling motion, leaning out over the side of my harness. I took both steering toggles in one hand so I could drag the other hand through the air, like an eagle's wingtip.

Was I turning, or was it the earth I had caused to spin beneath me? Weren't we all spinning around the sun, and the sun spinning with the solar system within the Milky Way? Amid all this spinning, who could tell what was stationary, who was moving? From my viewpoint, as the centre of the universe, everything was revolving about me.

"And look!" I marvelled to myself, "if I cross the thermal and turn the other way, I cause the earth and everything to spin in a new direction!" I laughed, full of wonder, trailing my hand through the air.

The thermal slowed after 1500 metres of climbing, because it had cooled along the way. Having lost its buoyancy, the narrow current had begun to widen and weaken, mixing with the outside air. A few circling turns were all that was left of my ride, the once-youthful thermal had found a peaceful old age. I glided off to find a new partner in my aerial ballet.

I spotted the first signs of a cumulus cloud. As the cloud built, it drew in air from beneath it. The trick was to find the originating thermal and ride it up to the base of the cloud, where the lift was abundant.

I felt the sudden rush of air. "Beep! Beepbip!" my variometer chirped away to itself, happy to be singing a rising tune. I flew straight for a while, trying to establish how wide the thermal was. After ten seconds of steady climbing, I banked around to circle in the lift. The thermal was smooth and wide. I eased back in my harness and looked up at my wing. The fabric was a brilliant cascade of colours - a great yellow span, a violet leading edge, indigo inside the cells.

Flying was an invisible kind of art, I mused, carving around in a wide turn. I made broad strokes and graceful spirals upon the vast canvas of air, leaving no trace of my art behind. I was the artist and the only likely observer.

My brushstrokes took me circling up towards the growing cumulus cloud. It was spreading out in the sky above my wing. I levelled out of the turn. We continued to climb, slowly. I tried to gauge how far above me the cloud was. I didn't want to climb too high and get sucked into it.

Inside a cloud it is cold and wet, so you become soaked. You also become disorientated, because you have no reference points. The sun becomes a diffused light-source. The ground disappears from view. Soon you become unsure of where the horizon is, whether you are turning left or right or not at all. This can lead to frantic feelings as you battle to escape the cloud. And once you are enveloped in the cloud, it is quite possible that the cloud will continue to grow, with you inside it. If it is a day when thunderstorms are building, then you really have a problem, for the baby fluffy cloud you entered can grow into a fully mature thunderhead quickly. Then the real ordeal begins. For thunderstorms are the most fearsome beasts in the free-flying realm.

Thunderstorms have been known to tear the wings off aircraft. The updraughts become so strong in places that you could be freefalling without a wing and still be sucked upwards. Hailstones the size of tennis balls fly around within them. Lightning flashes inside the cloud. The thunder would blow your ears out. You would freeze solid as you were hoisted higher and higher, so high that the air is too thin to breathe. And the turbulence could thrash your paraglider so violently that you could be swung above it, tumbling through the lines to fall into the wing and so plummet to the earth. It would be one hell of a ride, but it would be your last.

Or at least this is what my instructors told me when I went to flying school.

Don't go into cloud, they said. Don't ever go in, it's so dangerous. 'Dangerous' is the kind of word you remember. I had always remembered about clouds, and feared the moment when one day I might get sucked up into that dark and dreaded misty chaos. So I scuttled out and away from the cloud before I was at its base. You can never be sure how strong the lift would eventually become. It was kind of fun though, teasing the cloud and then racing away.

The mountains fell away, folded in wonderful grey-green shapes beneath me. I explored slowly down the range, circling beneath the forming clouds and running away again, breathing in the crisp, clean air. The sky gradually began to fill with the clouds, clouds that bulged higher and higher, billowing outwards.

It was probably time to return to the ground, I thought. Any moment soon there would be a thunderstorm raising its head out of one of those clouds. I turned back towards my launch site, and pushed the speedbar out to the end of its pulleys, flying fast. I glided through a thermal, another, and another.

Something was wrong. On average I should be sinking, steadily burning off altitude with my steep glide angle. But I was still climbing, the climbs wouldn't stop. A whole section of the sky was going up.

Which could only mean one thing. I craned my neck to scan the sky above me. There was a lot of cloud off to the left, but it wasn't too big ... and then my heart stopped. To my right towered a huge cumulus cloud, a massive white cauldron of power. I had been dreaming, floating around, inebriated with altitude, and I had missed the developing danger. Silly, stupid, dumb. I reached up and tucked my wingtips in, which would make my wing smaller and so cause me to sink faster.

*Please, pleaseplease let me get down before this becomes a thundercloud. Just five minutes I promise I'll be on the ground. Just let me descend!*

Kada-booommmmm!

Too late, it was a thundercloud. I had very little time left to escape, maybe no time at all. I rolled hard to the right, spiralling into a dive. There was no time for half-hearted attempts. I needed to get onto the ground. Fast.

My stomach lurched as the G-forces increased. My variometer moaned in dismay as I plummeted, and the earth spun wildly around one motionless point in the centre of the spiral. My harness creaked under the strain.

*I hope it holds, if that goes there's nothing else between me and the ground.*

I found myself staring at my carabiners, the metal connectors that joined my harness to the glider. They looked too thin to bear the load. I groaned as the spiral dive tightened even further, forcing more G's, draining blood from my head and sending it towards my toes. It was too radical. I released the turn, and my glider fired out of the spiral, climbing up into the sky. The variometer screamed. Up! Up! Up! We were heading for the cloud at twelve metres a second.

There was no choice, I had to spiral. I yanked in the wingtips again, folding the wing to half its size, then banked hard to the left, and dropped into a sickening corkscrew spiral. At last the vario stopped beeping.

After what seemed like an age, I was near the ground, somewhere in the foothills. Boom! The thundercloud roared its anger at its brightly-coloured prey. It loomed above me, dark and ugly, with great curled towers up high. I scanned the landing area, trying to find some hint of which way the wind was blowing.

Strangely, it looked dead calm, despite the storm. I set up for a landing near the middle of the field, and swooped down.

I saw it rushing through the grass too late, coming from behind me - there was nothing I could do. Flying grass and debris hit my helmet, and my glider pitched forwards, below the horizon. I pulled sharply on the control lines, trying desperately to slow the dive, but I was already too low. I hit the ground hard, rolling awkwardly. My ankle twisted. I rolled in the dry grass and dived for my glider, catching it before it could drag me across the field in the wind. My right ankle was sore, I could feel it protesting in its boot.

The full force of the gust front hit me then, roaring across the field, trying to tear my glider out of my hands. Dust blew into my eyes. I bunched in as much of my wing as I could reach. If I had landed thirty seconds later it would have been bad. I lay on my glider until the raging wind had passed.

After cramming my glider into its bag, I pulled off my boot to investigate the damage. My ankle was painful, it throbbed within the joint, but I could move it from side to side. Nothing broken, just sprained. It would heal up if I rested it for a while. I had come away lucky.

A calm settled in the glen, and a faint sound caught my attention, a few notes of music. Or was I imagining it? I listened for a minute, but there was only the warning swirls of another gust front coming through the foliage. Then, another few notes of music, closer. A flute. The tune was somehow familiar. I felt that I should know where I had heard it before ... or who had played it. I watched where the sound had come from, but I couldn't see anyone there.

"You are supposed to land on the ground not in it!" boomed a familiar voice from behind me. I jumped, and Beagle laughed.

"Beagle! What are you doing out here?" I was glad to see him.

"I saw you spiralling down from the thundercloud and thought you might need a hand."

His presence puzzled me. The mountain club hut was over an hour away, up on the mountain. He wasn't even breathing heavily.

"But how did you get here so quickly?"

He smiled broadly. "I can move pretty fast when there is a need."

He hadn't moved fast, he had moved like lightning. Unless he'd been trekking for over an hour to where he had foreseen that I would crash. Maybe it was just coincidence. He must have already been in the area, for his own reasons.

"And play the flute at the same time?"

He grinned. "The music adds a spring to my step." He was in one of his cryptic moods, I was not going to get answers out of him. "Here, take it for a moment, would you?"

He hoisted my backpack onto his shoulders.

"You okay to walk?" he asked.

"It's going to be a mission to get back to the hut." I tested out my ankle and winced. I could walk about, slowly. Three, maybe four kilometres to the hut?

We set off at a hobbling pace. I used Beagle's shoulder for support until I found a sturdy walking-stick. The afternoon wore on. When the path came to the steep ascent into the mountains, I sat down to rest.

"I'm going to need a while," I called weakly to Beagle. "Unless you've got a magic carpet."

Beagle considered this for a moment, then shook his head. "I don't trust carpets. I'll push on ahead and drop your glider off at the hut. I'll be back soon." He was gone before I could protest. He was too generous.

I watched the thunderstorms building and linking with each other off to the east. It was going to rain within the next hour. It was hard going up the rocky track, but I hadn't gone far before Beagle returned to help me. At least this time he had some sweat on his brow.

That evening there was a heavy thunderstorm. It boomed above our hut, driving blue lightning into the peaks and bruising the ground with hailstones. The roof became a drum; the hail hammered upon the corrugated iron in a deafening drummer's roll. Beagle rushed outside with the water-bucket, and returned with a load of ice.

"You could do with some of this on your ankle," he said.

It was cold, but it felt good, in a masochistic kind of way. Beagle lit a fire in the stove and put the kettle on to boil. I realised that I had never asked him an obvious question.

"Do you fly?"

"Mmm. I've got a hang-glider, but I don't use it anymore. I've flown a few times with the eagles, but now I prefer to work with my mind."

"So you don't fly anymore?"

"I don't need a hang-glider to fly. The eagles take me with them. I learn with them, I follow their mastery of flying."

"But isn't that learning mostly instinctive? They don't have to learn that much."

"Oh no!" Beagle exclaimed. "You couldn't be more wrong. They must learn everything. Watch an eagle chick grow up, and you'll see it's a comedy of errors in the early days. They spend their whole lives learning, perfecting flying, mastering the Air."

"You can't master air," I disagreed, "it masters you. Look at me today."

"The eagles have taught me differently. By respecting its power, you can learn to guide your actions. Mastery lies in never putting yourself in a position where such a power can overwhelm you. Then you can use it for your own purposes."

"You're saying that I should have landed earlier?"

"With those wings? Yes. Acknowledge where your weaknesses are, fly with them in mind."

Fly according to my weaknesses, not my strengths? That was so limiting! It was the opposite of what I expected to hear from him. I bristled. As a paragliding instructor, I wasn't used to being criticised about my own flying.

"But if I did that, I'd never fly at all. I'd be too scared of breaking my weak little bones."

"That's fear," he disagreed. "That's different. Weakness is something you have because of what you are."

"And weaknesses can be worked upon," I suggested.

Beagle's face lit up. "Exactly! The eagles work on their weakest flying skills all the time. To challenge something without the ability or weapon to allow you to win is not brave, it is foolish. You may survive by luck a few times, but that is not mastery. If you simply believe you can achieve everything, acknowledge no fear, and have no respect for forces greater than you, if you try to fly everywhere, in any conditions, regardless of the consequences, well that is a short path to an untimely end. If you fly with respect, you never cease to observe yourself and where you are in relation to the forces that are present."

"That destroys the freedom!" I objected. "If you are always analysing where you are, where the clouds are, where the wind is, how much height you have, it invades your mind with technical thoughts. It's like what you said about your mind being too full of mental chatter. All I want to do when I have altitude is to relish it, to immerse myself in the beauty of the sky, without distraction, without thinking. If I ran a monologue of analysis all the time, it would destroy that freedom. There would be no release in the flight, no joy."

"You misunderstand me. I didn't say analyse, I said observe. Do you remember the eagle's perspective?"

The eagle's perspective: vision, separated from sight, the projection of awareness. "Of course I remember it. What's your point?"

"You can use that skill to be aware of things, to watch yourself and the powers at play. As you extend yourself further, you face greater danger. You must be alert to the movement of power around you. It is a basic principle of self-defence. It comes from truly having respect for the element you are exploring."

"What makes you such an authority on flying?" I asked him cagily. He was right. But I hadn't asked for a lecture.

"Ten years of being an apprentice to the eagles," he responded.

"And an old hang-glider you don't know how to fly," I added, with a wink.

"I'd fly it better than you fly your mattress, it would seem," he answered, seeming to take no offence at my ribbing. "You've still got a lot to learn, you probably haven't even come across the Sink Monster yet."

"The Sink Monster?"

"See, I knew it! Sink, as in 'falling out of the sky' not as in the kitchen fitting. I'll tell you about the Sink Monster after supper. If you eat all your vegetables." He laughed and danced out of the way of my backhanded swing.

So I was to get a bedtime story. I had a feeling it was to be a tongue-in-cheek tale.

\* \* \*

For aeons the Sink Monster lurked, hidden from sight, out of knowledge, in a forsaken forest of black and tortured trees in a land that had not yet been named. It could not see the shape of its own body, and it cast no shadow on the ground, but it knew that it was powerful. Very powerful indeed. As time passed, it saw that it was shackled to the ground by its nature, while things moved above, up on high. Free things, floating things. The Sink Monster grew jealous. It grew angry.

A puff of white vapours was enjoying the exhilaration of becoming a cloud. The sensation of growing was strong. More and more moisture was climbing into its belly, releasing energy. The cloud formed crisp edges; it rose into a towering mass that shadowed huge tracts of land in the world below, including a forest of black trees. The cloud felt a cold and heavy fear. Something was down there, something evil, something mean.

The Sink Monster watched the rising cloud, going up and up into the sky. It must be torn apart, it must be shredded and beaten until it fell to the ground, for nothing should be allowed to be so free!

The Sink Monster tore it down. The poor little thundercloud lashed back with lightning, and it roared with thunder, but the Sink Monster was mightier. All that was left of the cloud were the tears that fell to the earth as rain.

And the Sink Monster was satisfied. It had found its purpose. It would tumble things from the sky, just to see them fall and to hear their screams. A millennium passed, then a few more, and the Sink Monster stalked across the face of the earth, looking for prey. There was good hunting in the mountains, where the clouds were hasty, and the falls were greater. But even so, the Monster was still angry. The clouds did not satisfy his appetite any more.

The Sink Monster saw things climbing in the trees, and so he shook the forests, and the monkeys fell down. The monkeys became too afraid to climb up high. They began to ask questions, and they became mankind. The Sink Monster lost interest in them. Until, one day, a man built a device, and he stepped into it, and he flew.

The Sink Monster raged. It should not be. The monkeys had found freedom, and he could not join them. At first they flew in wooden boxes, then in metal ones, and then they grew even braver and flew with just a floppy curve of fabric over their heads.

The Sink Monster shivered with anticipation. So colourful and easy to see, with a noisy alarm to signal which one was rising the fastest, so many of them, and oh so easy to crumple up and beat down toward the ground! The Monster reached out an invisible claw, and shredded a bright green glider.

"Aaaaai!" shouted the monkey as it spiralled downward. The Monster noticed that if you kept batting it from one side, the glider would fall faster and make more noise. Until it crashed into the ground, when it was no fun anymore.

All the other gliders came down then, out of the sky, to look at their fallen friend. Some took him away, hoping he could be healed, while the others stood around and discussed the event.

"It was his fault," the one said.

"The glider! The glider! Send it back to the manufacturer!" said another.

"It was the wind, it came out of nowhere."

"It was the wrong time of day to be there."

"No, he should have counter-steered with his left hand and tied the lines together with his right hand while he threw his parachute with his foot."

"He was unlucky," someone else said quietly.

Then they all chanted, "Pilot error, pilot error, pilot error," and went up their hill again. They'd soon be out again, beeping and turning upwards toward the clouds, in a way that made the Monster furious.

The faster the gliders climbed, the more violent the Monster became. The closer the gliders flew to the rocks and other gliders, the easier it was to cause them to fall.

So when you are turning skywards, remember that the Sink Monster is out there. Nothing has changed. He will get around to you, he's simply busy on your friends. You can't beat him, no matter how good you are. You can only run away, so fly with a bit of space to deal with his fury. Otherwise we'll miss you, friend, and they'll all chant, "Pilot Error."

# LIFE-FORCE

The next morning I awoke late. The sun was blazing. It was already hot, the vegetation had a dry look to it, heat shimmered on the stark, rocky cliffs. The wind shook the bushes until they swung wildly. It was not going to be flyable.

Beagle was gathering his possessions together and loading his backpack.

"Good morning!" he muttered.

"If it is a good morning, that is," I mocked his lack of enthusiasm.

"I am leaving today," he explained, "Now, actually."

"Why so?"

"I have just been up to visit the eagles. They accepted me in their thoughts only long enough to tell me that I should study silence. Then they linked their minds again, and bonded. They are mates now, for life! And I was excluded, once again. I won't learn any further with them, I must find others. I will go south, deeper into the mountains; maybe there I can find some free eagles."

I didn't know what to say. I felt I would lose so much if he left, but I had no reason to ask him to stay. We each had our own lives to live, our own journeys. I couldn't ask him to hang around just because I found him interesting.

"Do you think I'll see you again? Do you have a contact address so I can get hold of you sometime?" I never have been very good at goodbyes, especially with friends.

"A contact address!" Beagle snorted. "What a novelty that would be! I am where I am, which is not where yesterday was nor tomorrow shall be." He laughed. "But your world is far smaller than you think. We shall meet again, because we are doing the same thing, studying the freedom of the sky."

It was sad to say goodbye so soon. I had enjoyed Beagle's humour. "Well I really enjoyed meeting you," I said sincerely, offering my hand. He clasped it in a firm handshake.

"You have been a delight," he said warmly. "Until we meet again."

"Good luck. I hope you find the right eagle." I knew it was a weak farewell, but I was at a loss for words.

"You'll be an eagle-friend one day," he said, then he walked out. I watched quietly from the door. He strode down the path, the wind tousling his hair. He walked away, growing smaller until he was out of sight. He didn't turn back once.

A strange man, I thought to myself, missing him already. I had never met someone quite so determined to follow his own calling, so self-sufficient and so mysterious. He had left on his own mission, and I was left to mine.

I leaned back against the wall, feeling alone. What was my mission, anyway? What was I doing out here, away from my friends and family, away from society? My twisted ankle throbbed. I hobbled off to make some breakfast, and yelped with pain when I put too much weight on my foot. Blast it! Why had I gone and crashed, the day before? Why hadn't I done something safe, like hiking? Why did I have to fly at all? Was the view really that good, that it justified the risk to life and limb?

Why risk your life, risk your body, risk your friends and risk your money to fly, I wondered? Why? Why throw yourself off a mountain slope tied to a flimsy canopy of cloth? Why?

Why turn through the turbulence, turn in the thermal to be lifted up above the earth, up high into the clouds, into the thin cool air where all is crisp and fresh? Why?

Why fly away from your known world, fly over new mountains, new fields and valleys far below, with new sky all around you, whistling through your lines, new winds to be blown by, unknown landings in faraway places? Why?

Why spend your time not on Earth but above it, letting it turn below you with its seductive comforts? Why fly, never losing hours in the television's ghostly glare, never losing mornings to lethargic late-starts, to never know boredom? Why?

Why spin upon high on a wing, with the pure joyous feeling of being alive and in the air, looking down in rapture, feeling your spirit soar, passing through winds and clouds and up, ever higher, until you feel you are almost a part of that big, big sky?

And so in asking, I was answered.

Flying was my quest, a realm of challenge and self-discovery. To live without flying would be to live without passion; to merely exist. I imagine that once you have flown, it is impossible to ever truly give it up.

With flying in my life, there was constant growth, I was faced with challenges that demanded that I improve myself, lest I get hurt. The danger was a necessary element. Without the danger, the experiences would lose their relevance. Because if I couldn't get hurt, the fear would not be present.

Without fear there would be no limitations to break through. Everything would be immediately possible. To merely move about in the sky in an entirely safe vehicle would be pretty, but boring. It would be just another form of transport. But flying! That was something completely different.

Each airborne moment was so intense. Each fear was real and had a reason. To transcend those fears required a considered approach. The fear pointed to a danger that needed to be acknowledged, but it didn't have to be a limitation. If I could identify the danger I feared, then I could work on developing the necessary skills to master the danger. Finally I could move on, unhindered by the fear.

So my mission was to fly. But for the moment, I had to wait, grounded by my injury.

The hut was silent. I sang to fill the emptiness. The song came out flat, not even reaching to the walls, and my voice trailed off. I pushed some wood strips into the ashes of the stove. The crumpling of paper in my hands was almost deafening; the strike and flare of the match was loud. The flames licked through the paper and the wood began to hiss.

When I stood up to fetch water, shooting pains ran up my leg. I favoured my good ankle and hopped out of the door.

The glare outside made me squint. It was a scorcher of a day. I filled my billycan from the stream, and watched the bubbles swirl in the water. I wondered what I should do with my time. I couldn't fly, not on my damaged ankle. Besides, it was too windy. Maybe I could write a story, but I wasn't really in the mood. Writing needed a certain lucid sensitivity and I was feeling rather dull and empty-headed.

The cool water felt nice on my hands. I remembered a waterfall and pool I had seen, probably half an hour's walk away. If I took it easy I could make it there and back.

The sun beat down on me, on my way to the waterfall. The leaves curled, the air shimmered in waves. I made good speed, moving with three steps and a hop. Sweat stuck my shirt to my skin.

As I dropped down from a large rock I disturbed a crow which had been perched nearby and it flapped its large oily-black wings reluctantly to escape. It shot me a sidelong glance once it had landed.

"Son of Satan," I scolded the crow.

It cocked its head and then hopped along parallel to me. The crow mimicked my gait, with three short hops and then one great leap, three short hops, one great leap.

We made a comic couple. I burst into laughter.

"Begone!" I shouted at it.

The crow gave one ebullient "Skrraaaak," and retreated to a safe distance.

A dull roar approached. I could taste the moisture in the air, that fresh scent of tumbling, evaporated water. The air was cooler, drawing me irresistibly towards the waterfall.

A dark, clear river flowed out of a gorge, and there the path turned. I hobbled off the path and followed the river downstream, towards the thunder.

The falls were impressive. Wisps of vapour curled restlessly above the water, just beyond the edge of the falls. A rainbow danced in the haze, steady despite the twisting air currents. The river narrowed and flowed fast over the falls, where the wind tore at it, creating a sparkling mist. There was a deep, dark pool, far below, rimmed with creamy-white foam. The pounding of the water resounded off the cliffs.

Downstream, the river shallowed again and rocks were visible under the surface of the water, but the pool itself was dark and mysterious, a deep chasm.

The deafening roar was strangely envigorating. It felt as if the waterfall vibrated deep within my body, in my bones. I breathed in a draught of the moist and vital air. I spread my arms out and leant forwards on the edge of the cliff, as if I was going to launch myself off and dive into the pool far below. But I was just stretching, feeling the wind on my arms. It was too far down to jump.

Although, it was a clear jump - the cliff was sheer and the pool was more than big enough.

No, it was lunacy.

"Lunacy," I repeated to myself, stepping back slightly from the edge. My pulse was racing - how silly, I wasn't even going to jump and was all keyed up. I would have to find the path that led down to the pool, and walk down for a swim.

*When you jump you might as well keep your boots on.*

"I am not jumping off this cliff!" I protested nervously at my inner voice.

*Fear?*

"No, I'm not scared. Just, it's too far down and I'll kill myself."

Well, I wouldn't really kill myself, it wasn't that high. I leant out over the edge again, to gauge the height of the drop. It was a long way down. There were butterflies in my stomach. I was scared of it.

*Acknowledge it.*

"Okay, so I'm scared. It's a natural survival instinct."

*Understand it.*

I sifted through alternative sources of fear that presented themselves to my mind. Fear of death? No, that wasn't really a concern, it was highly unlikely. Fear of injury? Partly true, I didn't know how hard the water would hit me, but that also didn't really account for the racing pulse. Fear of letting go? Letting go of control? That was at the heart of my distress.

For once I had stepped beyond the edge, I would have no control. There would be a few seconds there where I would be purely at the mercy of gravity, the outcome determined by chance. Would I hit the water straight? I was confident that I could handle the swim at the bottom. It was just the letting go of control that scared me.

Bah! I had come for fun, for enjoyment! Be damned if I was going to ruin it by having to battle through some fear. The pool was down below, and I was going swimming. I hopped away from the falls, back towards the pathway.

The cold water was glorious, when I finally reached it. I floated for a long time on my back, paddling lazily. The current pulled me around. The resonant roar of the falls energized me. I sank slowly below the surface, then rose again, feeling the warm air on my skin before sinking back into the cold water. The cold had numbed the dull pain in my ankle, and without having to support my weight it was free from strain.

I watched the clouds tumble into wonderful shapes in the deep blue sky. There seemed to be no limit to the sky's extent and I felt that if I could just reach out far enough, I could touch the sky. A cloud like a magic lamp floated by on the wind. With a little bit of thought it became a goldfish. I wondered if I could make the cloud disappear, like Richard Bach did in *Illusions*.

I puffed out my cheeks and blew through my pursed lips. At the same time I tried to imagine that I was the cloud, felt myself curl in misty white, rolling with the air. Then I allowed myself to dissolve, imagined the future of a clear blue sky. Slowly and gloriously, the future became the present, and the cloud was gone!

"Did you see that?" I congratulated myself. "I did it! I made a cloud vanish!" The logical side of my mind was screaming blue murder, but the creative side rejoiced in the new-found freedom.

I had to do the vanishing trick again, just to see if it was real.

There was a really big cloud that drifted all by itself. Maybe it was too big, maybe it wouldn't work the second time and then I wouldn't be sure if I really could perform magic ever again. I didn't want to spoil my daydream by proving myself wrong. I was happy, I knew I could make clouds vanish.

Could I, really?

The large cloud had grown. I looked at the cloud and concentrated hard, but it took a lot of fffff and there wasn't much POOFF. I kept on and on at this cloud until it looked like it was becoming smaller, but I couldn't be sure. The harder I thought about it, the more difficult the task seemed to become, as if the more I struggled with forcing the cloud to disappear, the more it became a real object in the sky. By straining to make it vanish, the cloud was becoming an object worthy of strain, bulging ominously along its edges, darkening in moist defiance. I was not succeeding. I changed tactics then, trying to repeat my earlier imperious dismissal of the cloud, as if it were not an item worthy of so much attention.

"Begone!" I commanded and let go of my thoughts of vanishing clouds, allowing the thoughts to dissolve in my mind as I wanted the cloud to do. The feeling of allowing seemed to be a key, for as I allowed the cloud to dissolve in my mind, my reality began to transform. The cloud slowed in its development, then the bottom cleared up and the side became translucent, then the haze was gone and I had made the second cloud vanish.

The logical half of my mind rebelled. There had to be a mistake, there was no way that things could just vanish like that, it would be magic and magic didn't exist. Magic was a fantasy, caused by illusions and sleight of hand. Magic did not belong in the real world.

*Maybe magic is the real world,* answered my inner voice. *The world of logic could be the illusion, a flawed attempt to understand what is a mystery.*

I floated for a while longer, considering such things.

When I climbed out onto the bank a stab of pain reminded me of my incapacity.

"Damn you!" I chastised my ankle, "why can't you just heal up!"

The thought struck me. If my ankle needed healing and magic was real, then why not use it to heal myself, dissolving the damage just like the clouds? There were many reports of healers who performed miraculous cures. If they could do it, then the possibility existed.

I sat on the bank and drew my injured leg towards me so that my ankle lay across my lap. I let out a long breath, and tried to perceive exactly what the matter was with my ankle. Which ligaments were torn, which tendons stretched, where was the joint damaged? I gazed at my leg, drifting in my mind. But I could perceive nothing, and I had no idea of what to do next. All very well to decide to heal with magic, I thought, but how?

*Use the eagle's perspective,* chimed my inner voice.

My inner voice seemed to have an answer for everything. If part of me was so damn evolved, I wondered, then why did I have to struggle on, making mistakes and losing my way?

*The answers are all there,* replied my inner voice, *but you only grow by discovering the questions.*

I stared out defiantly across the pool. Eagle's perspective, indeed! Separating my vision from sight wouldn't help me to heal my ankle. A mere change in perspective would not ...

A change in perspective. Of course! The eagle's perspective was not only about soaring above the ground! Beagle had used his movable point of perception to see objects outside the hut, behind him, around him. Why not within him, too?

I gazed at my ankle again and concentrated on shifting my awareness. The waterfall roared in my ears. My vision grew hazy, then suddenly I was inside my ankle, moving over tendons and around the bony growth of the joint. Before me stretched the ligaments of my calf muscles, a thousand fine fibres patterned in parallel tension. I moved slowly around the ankle, scanning the images that flooded my mind, looking for something that looked unnatural, some disturbance in the strangely co-ordinated patterns of human tissue. Nothing seemed out of place. Then I saw it, a broad area of purple-black tissue below the ankle, nestled around the heel. The cells were bruised and emitted a dark discomfort. There was the source of my pain.

To heal it I would have to transform that darkness into clean, living cells. Not much different to transforming a white cloud into blue sky. As long as I remembered not to think too hard about the bruises but rather the end result, the healthy future, things should work out fine.

I visualised the damaged cells sparkling with a healing light, pulsing with strength and vitality. I allowed the darkness of the injury to dissolve, softening like the dying remnants of the cloud.

The only problem was, part of me knew that people didn't just go around and heal themselves with magic. It was not possible. Or not right. Or something. I managed to reach a compromise that didn't threaten my logic too greatly, by healing myself partially, leaving a thin trace of bruising deep in my heel.

I stood on both feet, testing the improved mobility of my ankle. I had succeeded, although if challenged I would be able to argue that it was the effect of the pool and walking and maybe it hadn't been all that sore in the first place. I wasn't quite ready to step into a world ruled by magic, but I had taken a step away from iron-bound reason.

All was not as it seemed, in my world.

Maybe fears are like the clouds, I thought. The more realness we give them by trying to fight them, the more realness they take on. The clouds were easy to dissolve because I did not think of them as solid. The rocks and trees and pool around me were a different matter altogether.

Although atomic physicists have told us that everything is made up of a large amount of space and a few spinning particles of energy, I found it difficult to perceive the truth of this. To me, the tree beside the pool was a solid, living object. It was real, and because I perceived it as real, it remained in my world and resisted my attempts to make it disappear.

In the same way some fears took on a realness of their own. They were, in reality, only clouds. A fear, when given realness by my indulgence, took on a substance and became a fact of life. Like my fear of releasing control, I realised. By climbing down from the waterfall, I had added a little more realness to my fear. The defeat had already shaped my world to exclude the possibilities that lay beyond the fear. The next time that I was confronted with a possibility of losing control, I would react timidly, without confidence, for I would remember my defeat.

And so the fear became part of the world that contained me. The experiences beyond it were inaccessible, unseen and increasingly unreal. Not being able to perceive beyond my limitations, I would believe them to be real and believe that my experiences were all that there was to life.

To make a cloud vanish, I had to *allow* it to go.

I scrambled up the path to the top of the waterfall, wearing only my boots. The sun dried the water from my naked body. My heart trip-hammered in my chest. Surely I wasn't going to jump off the cliff, it was too high, the pool was too far below, my body too defenceless in the fall.

I leapt across the rocks to the edge of the fall. *Master the forces,* echoed my inner voice. I breathed in the fresh vapours, and stepped onto the last rock. To be out of control involved trusting in life. I had to believe that I would survive, regardless of whether I was in control or whether I was out on a limb. A leaf flowed past in the current and rushed off the falls. I looked down into the chaos of white foam sparkling in the sunlight at the base of the falls. I simply had to release my need for control to get there.

*Go beyond your fear.*

My legs were shaking. I slowly arched my body and spread my arms, stepping to the edge of my jutting rock. Thoughts flooded my mind in the seconds before the jump.

Why do I risk it? Why push the limits back at all costs, living on the edge, acknowledging this and pushing further and harder?

My heart pounded in my chest and I drew a ragged breath. I knew it was going to be my last.

ohnoiamgoingtojumpthisisit

mylegsaresinkingtighteningpushingleaping

I am

airborne!

I fell in a haze of vapours cast off the thundering waterfall.

I know I shall live, I am too alive to die.

Wham!

I laughed from deep inside, laughed hard and free as I came up from the depths of the pool to the surface. My skin stung where I'd struck the water, that barrier that had been such a limitation. I had done it.

Every cell in my body was tingling. I felt alive.

I had broken past my limits, into what lay beyond.

# VISUALISATION

One million leaves, sharing one Life-force -
Gold-yellow silhouettes amid cooling sky;
silverthread cobwebs run eager adventurers
from one curving bough to the air passing by.
Sunlit to brilliance a red leaf tumbles
through delicate branches its death but a sigh;
green younger brothers smile up to the Sun
their task not yet done, they breathe up on high.


The leaves scattered in my wake as I drove towards the Wild Sky Paragliding centre. The driveway was an avenue of oaks that rustled in the morning breeze. It had been an adventure all on its own just to find the place, tucked away as it was in the forest reserve, out of Bulwer town. The air was filled with the fresh scent of the forest. A squirrel bounded across the road and scampered up the nearest tree in mock terror. The dappled sunlight flickered over me as I drove towards the large homestead. I had a good feeling about this place.

Hans Fokkens, my host and a fellow paragliding instructor, was out in the garden, working on a trailer. He was wearing a sarong and his hair hung down his back in a dark pony tail. He sidled over to my car as I rumbled to a halt, leaning his tall frame against the fence. The peaceful quiet of the idyllic surrounds settled upon me as the engine died.

"Well hello, how pleasant of you to pop in!" Hans greeted me with a broad smile and hearty handshake. "What brings you here?"

"Its my very own Renault 5."

He rolled his eyes. "What are you doing in Bulwer?"

Why did anyone come to Bulwer? "I've come to fly. I've been on the road for seven weeks now, and thought I might visit for a while."

"Well, you're welcome to stay with us for as long as you want," Hans offered. "Have you seen our new place before?"

The 'new place' was an aged colonial-style house with a low roof and lots of charm. A wide terrace surrounded the house, proving ample space for relaxing and watching the world go by. Three wicker chairs, two log benches and a hammock were out on the terrace doing just that.

The house had many rooms, and polished wooden floorboards that creaked when you walked on them. The lounge was filled with furniture made from roughly-hewn wood. A few casual artworks hung on the walls, vague forms on silk. I knew at once that I could relax here. I could sprawl on the couch, I could lie on the floor with my shoes off, I could probably even sit on the coffee table.

The room contained memories of evenings spent telling tales around the fire, of travellers voices, and laughter.

A woman walked in with a blonde-haired child in her arms. She had a friendly face, soft green eyes and a halo of red-brown hair. She wore a colourful tie-dyed dress. The child regarded me with wide eyes, as if I had just walked in with no clothes on. Then she buried her head in her mother's breast.

"Don't worry, she's just shy. I'm Bridgette, and this is our baby Skye," she greeted me.

I returned her greeting, feeling welcomed. "Nice to meet you too, Skye," I added, trying to see her hidden face. She peeped out for a moment, then buried her head again, determined to be invisible.

"I see she has learned to play hard to get," I joked. "How old is she now?"

"Almost two," Hans said proudly. "I've started to teach her paragliding, she's been up in the air with me and loves it! Don't you Skye?" He took Skye and hoisted her into the air above his head, catching her gently and hoisting her upwards again. Skye gurgled.

"How long have you been here?" I indicated the house and forest.

"Oh, about a year now," Bridgette replied.

"We were very lucky," Hans added, "we are renting it from the forestry company. It is one of the few houses in this reserve and we love it. Life out here away from town is wonderful."

I could well believe it.

Bridgette showed me my room and I brought a few essentials in from the car, packing them next to my bed.

"Any other people staying here at the moment?" I asked.

"Only a few," Bridgette replied. "There's Josh, Paulo and Tom, who are staying in the other room and then Marguerite who's camping."

I hadn't seen anyone around. "Where are they now?"

"They're all out flying. " She waved in the general direction of the mountain.

Somebody was flying, and I wasn't there! I had to leave at once!

"Where? How do I get there?" I blurted out. "They're flying?"

"Relax, it's always flyable here," laughed Hans. "I'll take you round to the takeoff site. I've got to go into town to buy some supplies anyway."

I was in his car with my glider before he had crossed the grass.

The way up to the takeoff site at Bulwer was a winding dirt road that took us on a long detour through the forests behind the mountain. Being a forest road, there were parts that threatened to pull the exhaust from the bottom of Hans's car. He couldn't have driven fast enough for me.

There were five gliders airborne, floating about in the smooth ridge-lift. One glider was circling high above the others. A few clouds were building far out near the horizon.

The launch site was fantastic. Dry grass stretched out before me, covering the crest of the hill, spreading away to the left and right and sliding down the slopes in a carpet of pale velvet. No rocks, no bushes, no trees in the way, slopes steep enough to provide good ridge lift yet gentle and forgiving, and down in the valley waited the large landing field, a descent of some two hundred metres to the sleepy-hollow town of Bulwer.

To the north-west, a few peaks rose high above the grassed plateau. "We sometimes take off from the top of the peak, but usually you don't need to, you can just fly up there from here!" said Hans.

I liked the sound of that. Why walk, when you can fly? Soon I was airborne, rising on the wind, up towards the high mountains.

It was a spectacular vantage point.

\* \* \*

*Some skies are like the sea*
*and I a dolphin wild and free.*
*Cool currents well up from the keep,*
*lifting dark from the oceans deep.*
*I cut across reefs, and adamantine,*
*where waters hold a turquoise sheen*
*that shimmers light around my head.*

*A wash of creatures from the seabed*
*float by bright colours and fantastic frills*
*and below, the great green tumbling hills*
*become the ripples in a beautiful sand,*
*an emerald floor in a translucent land.*
*I swim upwards and wonder where I'll be*
*when I break through the surface of this strange and magic sea.*
*My circles take me ever higher and in joy I roll and play*
*and spiral swirling patterns, and pause to watch the way*
*the sunlight filters down in a golden shaft*
*parted by the drifting clouds, or are they shoals, or fishing craft?*

*And when the wind is wild and foul,*
*when it whips the sky to a frothy scowl*
*of dark grey and driving sprays' commotion*
*then I sink down deeper in my ocean*
*down to the seaweed of tall trees*
*to the calm of soft and sandy lees*
*between the rocks and shipwrecks bent*
*and there I hide in solace and content*
*until the wind has calmed the blue again*
*and the sea is smooth in my domain.*

\* \* \*

As we set off to Hans's house that evening, I noticed that my grin was mirrored on five happy faces around me. We had all enjoyed some of Bulwer's finest air. We were like merry wine-tasters who had tested an outstanding vintage for a little longer than was strictly necessary. We all talked at once as we raced along the dust road in Tom's Land Rover.

We congratulated Josh on his first real soaring flight. We laughed as Tom recounted his disastrous takeoff run which had ended with him rolled in his glider, just behind the windsock. We ragged Paulo about being caught in the lifting currents beneath a large cloud. He had disappeared from view for a few minutes. Now that we were all on the ground, it didn't seem so dramatic, so we embellished the story shamelessly until it had gained its rightful proportions.

Back at the house, we burst out of the Land Rover and rushed in to claim the showers. Marguerite won, amid gales of laughter, because she escaped from the rough-and-tumble the boys became entangled in. We attacked the kitchen next, but were ousted by Bridgette who was making supper. I managed to sneak a hunk of bread with peanut butter before I was whooshed out.

Hans arrived with baby Skye on his shoulders. A game developed where we tried to hide from Skye and Hans and they tried to find us. We played it without intelligence, so there were many discoveries of hiding players accompanied with peals of laughter from Skye.

Finally we were all showered and dressed and considerably less manic. Bridgette had prepared a vegetable stew and rice, which filled the dining-room with wonderful scents. There was something about good flying that made me ravenous. A symptom of being inspired and fully alive after the elemental experience of fresh sky.

After supper we retired to the lounge. We sprawled in various postures of contented bliss. It was good to be together with like-minded people. I had been very much alone for the previous few weeks. There had always been another town beckoning, another mountain to fly, more sky to explore. But in Bulwer I realised that sharing the experience was very good for the soul. I thought I might indulge in some permanence for a while and let the sky come to me, instead of rushing off to find the sky.

"So you're a paragliding instructor?" Josh asked. I had been teaching for five years, on and off. "What's the secret of getting so high? I saw you today and you were far out in the valley, away from the ridge lift, but you were always so damn high. I couldn't get more than about one hundred metres above the ridge."

"Yes, I'd like to know that too!" said Tom. "I've got all the instruments, but they don't seem to work. I've got a GPS, a variometer, and a speed probe. How did you find the lift when I couldn't with all my instruments?"

"All that junk's weighing you down," said Paulo. "You just got too much technology on board, bru."

"We call him Tom Technology!" Marguerite joked.

We all laughed, and Tom Technology scowled in mock anger. He couldn't deny it, he had enough gadgets to sink a battleship. His Land Rover was filled with flying maps, sunglasses for cloudy days and other pairs for sunny days, two-way radios, extendible aerials, binoculars, a laptop computer, video camera equipment. He was glaring at the GPS unit in his hands, pushing the keys in a vain attempt to recall his flight track.

"How much do you know about visualisation?" I asked Josh.

"Visualisation? Like picturing something in your mind? I did a motivational course down in Durban, and it was all about visualising how you want to be. That was a huge inspiration. Got me confident enough to try paragliding!"

"Excellent! And the rest of you guys?"

Tom shook his head vaguely, Paulo shrugged.

"I used to do a little Yoga?" ventured Marguerite.

I nodded. "That's great, yoga involves meditation, and that'll begin to show you what is possible. Let's see. Imagine a pink elephant with purple stripes." The suppressed laughter confirmed that some of them had active imaginations. "Now visualise yourself standing on the back of this elephant, smell the smells, experience the emotions. Live that moment in the future. That is the difference between imagining something and visualising it. Imagination is a creation, but visualisation forms your reality." I had learned the truth of this at the waterfall.

"But they are both in my mind!" Marguerite objected. "How can visualisation influence what is real?"

"Bear with me for a moment. Think. Your brain receives millions of inputs every second, which are processed and filtered. Only the fraction of information that is relevant will be considered. But what is relevant? What information is important out of the flood of impulses you are receiving throughout the day?"

I looked at Paulo.

"Things about survival?" he suggested. "Like anything that could be a danger to me."

"Or where to walk so that you don't end up in the road in front of traffic," said Tom.

"Yes, and the goal is staying alive," I replied. "Think about what things you would notice if you were walking down a street during lunchtime."

"Well, anything that looks like food," said Marguerite.

"Great! Why do you think your brain is filtering that information out as being important?"

"Because I'm hungry," she replied. "I want to eat!"

"Which is another goal. Anything that appears in our world which has something to do with our goals is noticed and remembered. It goes beyond basic needs. Have you ever thought about a specific make of car you wanted? As soon as you decided exactly what car it was, your brain alerted you to every car similar to the one you wanted everywhere you went. You hadn't realised they had made so many of that damn car - but suddenly that car was everywhere!"

Tom smiled and nodded. "And now I have my Landy," he said.

"Most of us do not have precise goals," I continued, "so our brain selects goals from our dominant thoughts. It uses these to subconsciously filter the information. It pulls out the relevant impulses and discards the rest. By visualising your own goals, you set precise images to respond to. That allows your mind to focus on the things that are occurring in your world that will bring you closer to your goals."

"But surely its the same thing?" asked Marguerite. "We think about the things we want?"

"Not always! We pick up goals from society without realising it. A newspaper headline about car hijacking makes us look suspiciously at strangers standing on the roadside. Advertisements stick in our mind. You didn't really want that can of soft-drink, and would have been quite happy until you saw the billboard, but now that you've seen it! The image keeps coming up in your mind, you see people around you drinking the drink, you look around to find out where they bought it from and POOF! all of a sudden you're standing there with a drink in your hand."

"Oh come on! Advertising doesn't have such a great hold over us!" Marguerite objected.

"We have a choice to ignore it, but if the thought of the soft-drink has made an impact and we make no conscious decision about whether we actually need it, we'll keep thinking about it, about the clever advert, and our brain will pick it up as a goal."

"What about if it's something we don't like, but we just can't get the thought out of our head?" Paulo asked.

"Same thing. When we focus on our fears and do not have any positive goals, these negative images endure and we begin to experience and attract to ourselves what we least want."

"You're saying we need to decide on our goals so that our brain can pick out the relevant facts in what we see," said Josh, leaning back on the couch, "but how do you use it with flying? There's nothing out there but sky. How do you visualise what you want when it's invisible?"

"To stand on the takeoff site and worry about dropping out is a big mistake. You are creating the sinking air for yourself. Your mind is now keyed onto 'sink' being a very important thing in your life. Your mind is simply performing its job, showing you where the sink is, and you'll find it everywhere."

"But that's natural, it's a fear," said Marguerite. "How do you change a natural reaction?"

"Take control of your thoughts!" I replied. "Think : I want to fly extremely high, up to the clouds. I am going to launch straight into a thermal. I can see myself turning lazy circles in the cold high air. I can feel the crisp wind on my face as I glide away from three thousand metres up. Now visualise the scene until you can see this future clearly in your mind. Feel the emotions and sensations of this vision. Make them as real as you can within your mind, involve all the senses - touch, taste, hearing, sight, smell, balance, movement. Add to these the joy of flying, the excitement you'll feel, the peace. The more adept you become at your visualisation, the more your brain will resonate with this intended future, each flight will become more of a success, closer to your visualisation until, one day, you shall be so precise that you can step into the visualised reality directly, like entering a magic window in your mind."

I stopped my monologue. I had said more than enough.

Paulo had fallen asleep on the couch. Tom glided a small paper plane off his knees and got up to fetch it. Josh nodded to me, but I couldn't tell whether it was just his way of trying to stay awake. Marguerite said nothing, she just hugged her knees close to her body. Well, at least I had tried.

Later, Tom told a story of his journey to South America. He'd been all over the Andes Mountains, looking for gemstones. We quizzed him until late in the night.

I had big dreams that night, soaring with birds of prey along a great mountain divide. I spoke to the birds with clear thoughts as we flew over massive cliffs and high, hidden villages. I could hear my own voice saying, "You can step into the visualised reality directly, like entering a magic window in your mind."

Was anything impossible, if one truly believed?

# THERMALSPOTTING

When I padded into the garden the following morning I was greeted with golden light that streamed down through the trees. The cool night air wafted out from the forest and brushed against my bare legs. I could smell the crunchy scent of bark, and the stickiness of tree-sap, the fragrance of the damp earth beneath distant ferns blended with the presence of green and growing things.

"It's flyable again," said Hans, sidling up behind me. "Want some breakfast?"

"Brilliant idea!" I replied. I joined the others indoors.

I should have gone hungry, and gone flying. By the time we arrived at the flying site, the wind was already too strong.

"Don't worry, it will die down, it always dies down," said Hans. He never allowed the weather half a chance to be unflyable, he was always out on the slope, ready to send his students off as soon as reality caught up with his beliefs. Unfortunately reality was still convinced that the wind was strong and no one had managed to convince it otherwise.

I wandered off along the ridge, in search of a sheltered vantage point from which I could enjoy the view of the waking day. I rested against a rock close to the edge of the ridge, and watched the landscape being a landscape for a while. I closed my eyes, drifting between wakefulness and sleep. The sunlight warmed me, my body grew heavy. I could have lain there all day.

I became aware of someone approaching. Tom was coming along the ridgetop. He had his GPS. Technology Tom.

"Mind if I join you?" he asked.

"Sure, you're welcome," I reassured him. "I was just daydreaming."

Tom sat down. "I wanted to ask you about what you said last night. How can I visualise myself into thermals when a thermal cannot be seen? I mean, it's invisible, a thermal, so how can I use the visualisation to draw me to something when I can't see it in the first place? What kind of picture do I visualise in my mind to create the correct goal? All I get is this glider floating about in nothing, going up."

"What would a thermal look like if you could see it?" I asked.

"Well, like nothing, a gust of wind, maybe a floating doughnut."

I looked out over the hills. "I see a shimmering multi-coloured heat-haze with a skin like an oil bubble."

"Hang on, are you suggesting that we can actually see these things?" I could see Tom was being careful, not wanting to appear gullible.

"Yes, and no. Have you ever looked at one of those stereogram images?" I asked him. "They were all the rage about two years ago. They have those computer-generated patterns all over them, gaudy colours."

"Yes," he said, remembering. "Those pictures you have to stare at for ages and then all of a sudden when you are looking in the right way you can see a three-dimensional image of a horse or a boat or something like that."

"They look like nothing until you focus your eyes at precisely the right place?"

"Yes. Oh, I see. You're saying that what I see contains a whole bunch of patterns like the stereogram, and when I learn to look in just the right way I will see the objects that are actually right in front of me but I can't see. Ahah!" He looked around with new eyes. "But can you ever really see the thermals?"

"Well, I think it works like this," I answered. "My mind builds a composite structure, full of movement, sound, colour and texture. To me, this is the world." I indicated the view in front of us, the mountain slopes leading out to the folded green hills, villages and roads. "And it *is* the world, but only as seen through my eyes. If a cat had to experience the same moment as I had, every object would have changed. A person would look different because the cat's eyesight is different. The person might have a fuzzy halo of energy, if it's true that cats can see auras. I'd probably smell bad, to the cat. The same objects become very different things. What about for dogs, beetles, butterflies, baboons? Each creature will have a different picture of 'the real world'. Who is to say which creature, with its own specialised perception, has the whole picture?"

Could we ever perceive our totality using our limited human senses, I wondered.

"But our senses are pretty good, aren't they?" Tom asked.

"Depends what you compare us to," I pointed out. "Compared to a mouse, we have great eyesight. Sharper smell than a frog. But compared to an eagle and a dog, we perform dismally. There is a huge amount of information that we just can't pick up. When I react to things that are happening in the world, I am really reacting to the inner picture I have built using my perception. And there are missing elements in that picture."

"So you're suggesting we can fill them in?" said Tom.

"Or pick them out of the trash. Things are discarded when the brain does not recognise the pattern in the barrage of stimuli. There is so much more out there, but we have an internal picture of 'the world' that contains only a few elements, those things we are 'trained' to see."

"So what do you do about it?" Tom asked pointedly. "How do you begin to recognise things that are being filtered out?"

"I close my eyes while I'm flying. That forces the filters to release their grasp because my brain needs every bit of information it can glean for survival. Then I try to visualise where the next thermal is. I fly there, and if I go up, I know I'm doing it right. This second sight is built from subtle senses. It is visualised into your internal picture of the world. The thermals slowly begin to emerge, before your eyes."

Tom's mobile phone rang loudly. He began to answer the call, then he scowled and turned the phone off.

"They always catch you at the wrong time," he muttered. "You were telling me about thermals. How long does it take before you can see the thermals like that?"

"Ah, don't get me wrong, I haven't mastered it yet, and I've been working on it for years. Some days I can see thermals, some days I see nothing but fresh air and on other days I think the whole idea is crazy. The less cynical you are, the more likely it is that you will be able to shift your perception."

We rested in silence for a while. A beetle crackled through the tangled grass-stems beside us. The beetle seemed to be taking an arduous path. Why didn't it just fly? It fell on its back, all four limbs waving in the air. I laughed and set the beetle right side up again.

"You're not normal," Tom commented.

"What makes you say that?" I played along.

"You're too happy."

"I just do the things that make me happy. Like flying. Living my dreams."

"But how do you make a living, just flying and adventuring? You have to make money."

That was the old fear that I'd left behind in the city. I wasn't going to argue with him. I'd stood behind that door for years. "I have simple desires," I answered. Being thrifty in the mountains wasn't a burden, it came naturally. When I had to carry everything around with me, I didn't want extra junk.

"I couldn't leave my job," he said. "I've got too many commitments."

We all choose our own commitments, I thought.

"You hold the key to freedom in your hand," I said.

He looked down at the cellphone, then back at me in surprise.

"Throw it away, and you have your freedom."

"Throw it away? Give up my job? And then what? Live off hand-outs?" He rose and stretched, bending the kinks out of his frame. "No, that's a bit too way out for me. But thanks for the pep talk anyway. I might be flying with my eyes closed next time, so you may find your own lesson flying back at you!"

I chuckled, and watched him saunter off along the ridgetop. He had just been ribbing me, but it did make me think. They say that you try to teach that which you most need to learn. Did I need to improve my vision, or my commitment to freedom?

I thought about the need to earn money. For me, money had been replaced by good fortune. Because I was happy, I had found a kind of harmony with the world. My days were full of lucky coincidences, as if my dreams had a way of providing for themselves.

When I had driven through the Eastern Cape, I had found good fortune. I was cruising along the back roads through the dry, deserted scrub-land, when suddenly my engine blew up. Or so it had seemed.

Smoke poured out of the bonnet, engulfing me in fumes. I lurched off the road and skidded to a halt, bursting out the door and running away, naked feet on the hot tarmac. I had expected the massive explosion that accompanies these scenes in the action movies. But reality can be surprisingly dull. The car just carried on smoking.

So eventually I summoned up the courage to wander over and lift the bonnet. Smoke billowed out. There were no flames inside, from what I could see, so I left the engine to cool.

A van veered off the road behind my car and came to a halt in a cloud of dust. The driver's door swung open, and a smiling face emerged. He had a shock of sandy hair. He approached and shook my hand with a firm grip.

"Vermeulen, aangename kennis."

I returned his greeting in English. My Afrikaans is *verskriklik*, but maybe Mr Vermeulen's English was worse. I left it up to him to decide which language to use.

"You having a braai?" Vermeulen indicated my car. "Come, I'll have a look."

I was relieved. I haven't got a clue which end is up in a car's engine. I know where the water and oil go in, but that's about it.

"Your head gasket's blown," came Vermeulen's voice from under the bonnet. "You're not going anywhere with this car. Where are you headed?"

"I'm just driving around, really, looking for a good mountain with a road running up it. I'm a paraglider pilot, so I fly off the mountains, sort of like ..." I made a vague, hopeless gesture with my hands, trying to demonstrate an aerofoil drawing a pilot below it from a mountain slope out into the sky. It is an impossible task to explain what paragliding is. How could you ever communicate the majesty of flight?

"*Jislaik.* You fly. So do I! I've got an old Apco, I fly off our mountain on the farm! Where do you come from?"

Of all the people who could have stopped for me, here was a pilot. We became instant friends, linked by the magic that ties all pilots into one family of enthusiasts.

Not only did he tow my car to his town, he also owned the garage there, so he fixed my car and he put me up for the week in his house. In return I trained him in cross-country flying and taught him the theoretical work he needed for his advanced paragliding licence. He had been waiting for months for the opportunity to improve his flying. Good fortune indeed.

If it had only happened once, I would have thought it was luck. But it happened all the time. There was a pattern to the coincidences.

I would reach a point in my journey where I didn't know what the next step was, where to go, but if I trusted in my dream, and stepped forwards, one of those lucky coincidences popped up. I've learned to persevere when things look uncertain. My fortunes always bring me the next stepping stone in the adventure.

I leant back in the grass and watched the blue heavens. The sky seemed fluid to me, never completely still, and yet it never went anywhere.

Up high, circling in the crystal fire of the sun, was one eagle, soaring on learned wings, transcending the world and its laws. I could fly too, I thought, I had my own wings. Could I reach the same height, would I find the same freedom? The beauty of it was that no matter how high I went, no matter how many limits I transcended, consciousness expanded and lessons learned, there was always another eagle circling higher on the thermal currents.

Eager shouts made me swing around. Hans was pulling up an old green-and-yellow glider in the slackening wind. He skidded across the ground for a while, then regained his footing and moved to the front of the takeoff area. He stepped into the air, effortlessly airborne. He soared away from the ridge, climbing steadily in the smooth lift. The pilots scrambled for their equipment.

Once I had unpacked my glider and readied all my kit, a constant breeze blew up the slope. Another perfect day for expressing my freedom. My glider swung in an arc as I pulled her from the ground, and she lifted me clear off my feet. Within moments I was circling in a buoyant thermal, watching the takeoff site sink away from my feet.

I closed my eyes and flew over the valley for a while, responding to the subtle images of my second sight. If I could use my inner vision to sense the thermals, I thought, then why not farther out, into space, beyond galaxies, beyond the stars, beyond things in the future, or the past?

My variometer began to beep just where I'd expected the thermal. I turned in the light lift and opened my eyes again. A cloud was forming above me. It was high and I doubted that I could reach it, but it made me think. If I could use the vision to find a thermal, maybe I could use it to fly through the cloud. My fear of clouds was based on a fear of losing my sight.

I relied on my sight to give me bearing and balance. It told me so much about wind currents, lifting air and turbulence. I was always looking down and around, collecting information, checking my position, watching my drift across the land, gauging how far I was from the rocks and cliffs.

Sight was the only sense that I really needed up there in the sky. I could hear the wind rushing through the lines of my glider and it filled me with peace. I could smell the freshness of the cool air and became invigorated by its taste. I could feel the soft pull of the wind on my clothing, through my hair, through the glider. All these sensations felt good but they just completed the flying experience. Sight was my only necessity.

I'd flown with my eyes closed, but I'd also known that I could open them at any time, should I hit turbulence. Going into a cloud would be very different. I would be altogether blind. And yet ... I knew where I was, in that internal picture, the world in my mind.

If I could develop enough trust in my ability, then I would be able to transcend the fear of losing my sight. I would be able to enter the cloud, to spiral wild circles into its cold, turbulent depths and emerge breathless from its sunlit heights.

I tried to climb up high, but I just couldn't climb high enough that day. The clouds remained always out of reach. I flew the lower levels; half man, half bird, limited by my abilities, soaring near the earth.

# A GOSSAMER THREAD OF FEELING

I played, in meditation, with a mirror. My reflection grinned as I reached out my hands to test its strength. Pushing against it I could feel the power of life within me. The mirror could not waver. I drew my hand away from the surface, pulling back, then swung my open palm into the mirror. SLAM! My reflection chuckled back at me, swinging its open palm out towards me at the same instant. SLAM!

We met with equal force at the boundary between real and unreal.

On such a day, I am strong.

I can visualise who I am, and so, I am.

But it is not always so, and it can be quite a trick to recognise the difference. The sun can be out, the wind can be gentle, but there's a chill within me.

It was just another day in Bulwer, a cloudless day. There were airborne gliders. My friends were in the air; there would be no problems. But the sky did not feel welcoming to me. Something was wrong.

I sat down for a while and munched on an apple. It seemed to calm me down. I savoured the clean mountain air. I waited, but when I reached for my glider, my stomach turned.

I spun around, expecting to see my airborne friends battling turbulence, their lives at the mercy of a great wind. All was quiet. A purple wing was gently thermalling high above takeoff, and dust from a passing car drifted away on the whispering breeze.

What was the matter with me? I was as jumpy as a cat in a thunderstorm. I didn't have a hangover, I wasn't sick. I was being a complete chicken. I had all the skills I needed to fly. I should be able to fly in any conditions. There was no need to back down. I had to fly! I didn't need to listen to the feelings of imminent danger.

My glider was too bright in the harsh sunlight. The wingtips fluttered restlessly as I laid it out on the launch site. I used both arms to lift the harness up and onto my body. It felt so heavy. My arms looked thin, just soft flesh wrapped about brittle bones. Why, with just a small force they could snap. I shivered. The sun glared down from on high.

A sharp gust jerked my glider off the ground. Quick, find the brakes! Pull them way back! Run with the glider! Whump! My glider fell back in place on the ground.

My heart was racing and my throat was dry. Deep breaths. The thermal had passed. The breeze caressed a blue streamer tied to a pole off to my right.

"Relax," I told myself. "Relax, r...e...l...a...x."

Slowly my heartbeat subsided. I prepared for the launch again. A little voice said something, but I couldn't make out the words. Five four three two one, it was time to go ...

Within all the excitement of the launch, there is a moment of focus when my awareness sharpens to a knifeblade. And in that moment I could hear it.

*Stop,* said a little voice from within. *Stop.*

The glider tugged on its lines, about to go. I should be feeling excited, but I felt as if someone had just walked over my grave. Slow footsteps crushed dry earth in a desolate place in my mind. The glider was going, tearing me away from the security of the earth, pulling me away into uncertainty.

I pulled the brakes to their stops. For an instant I hung, suspended, barely off the ground, caught in the moment of commitment. Then my wing crumpled in a stall, releasing me. My feet touched the ground once again.

I knelt down and touched the earth with my hands. The earth returned the touch.

After packing my glider away, I walked wearily away from the launch site. How would anyone understand why I didn't fly? How could I explain it to others, when I couldn't explain it to myself?

*Look in the mirror of your mind,* said my inner voice.

I found a quiet place, and I looked deep within, in meditation. I saw a pale reflection in the mirror. My reflection didn't smile as I reached out to test its strength. My hand sank into the haze. The mirror rippled and I felt myself dissolving. I felt my lack of vitality, my emptiness. There was darkness beyond.

I brought my awareness back to the warmth of the rock that my body was leaning against. I looked out at the world. Somehow my intuition had sensed that flying would have taken me close to the edge, too close for comfort.

I would rather miss an epic day than tempt disaster. My intuition had warned me by draining my will to explore, and dulling my passion for the sky.

Intuition may be a glimpse of the future, a brief instant of a world about to manifest. In following it, I avoided the impending danger, and so would never know what it had been. That's the mystery of intuition.

The more I listened to my intuition the clearer the messages became. Often it wasn't about avoiding danger, it was merely guiding me on a more fortunate path.

I took Tom's Land Rover and drove down into town, and the flow of intuitive impulses continued. My planned path was straight ahead, but I felt an urge to turn left at the first intersection. It was quicker to continue straight. Why turn left? There was no logical reason, left was simply the way of intuition, and straight ahead wasn't.

If I had driven straight, I would have reasoned it out something like this: I didn't have time to waste on vague notions. I had a plan for the rest of the day, and I wasn't going to have it disrupted without good reason. As I drove further on, I would have reasoned the intuition into ridicule. I was still alive, I hadn't encountered any horrible accident by going straight ahead, so my intuition must have been wrong. Such a silly thing, intuition, to make me want to turn left. There I was, on my way, fast and safe and according to plan. Intuition was a waste of time. After that little dialogue, my intuition would have been forgotten in the background of my thoughts, a vague urge that was never heeded, one that I'd be even less likely to heed in future. Intuition would vanish; there was no reason to remember it. Life would carry on, and I'd be the poorer for having never explored the road less travelled.

Instead, I turned left, on my way into town, following my intuition. I knew that I would now arrive at my destination at a different time, pass different people on the roadside, have different choices available to me.

A cow sauntered into the road and I came to a halt. A large black man approached my car, and knocked on my window. He was selling wire windmills, and he offered me one. I smiled and shook my head - I didn't need more junk.

But I caught myself. If I was there because of intuition, I should respond to the unexpected opportunities. I wound down my window and waved the man back. He was dressed in a long shirt of patterned African design. His feet were bare. His hair stood out in a halo of black curls. At his neck was a pendant of twisted seashells.

He smiled.

"You are the man who flies with the eagles."

I must have looked surprised, for he laughed. "You need a special one, bhuti, a special windmill." He danced off to his collection beside the road, and returned with the smallest windmill, one with bright blue and a jewel on the top. He leant in through my window, and I could smell the sweat and the fire. "This one tells you where to fly. Here, take it."

I held it in my hands, and watched the little blades spin, and the vane cock around, steering the windmill to face to the west.

"Hau!" he exclaimed. "You see? You must leave. You are needed in the west." He held my gaze with a frightening power. He seemed like a portal to an older, darker world.

He leant back, and the spell vanished. He was just a man with wire windmills. I paid him and he walked off as if nothing had taken place between us. I was too mystified to say anything at all. Then he was gone, and the cow moved off the road.

West, there was a whole country to my west.

Yet I knew at once where I should be.

# TRANSITIONS

As if by magic, the world changed around me; the one instant I was in Bulwer in the Natal midlands, the next I was staring out from my vantage high on the slopes of Table Mountain. A journey of almost two thousand kilometres had come and gone, the distance faded in memory. I was in the west.

The fresh wind carried rich scents of fynbos and sea. I was in Cape Town, my home town. It was hard to hold onto the dream of the Big Sky Life here, with the comforts of home so close by. But I still wanted to be alone in the sky, chasing my dreams, so I told nobody that I was home, and I avoided the city.

Cape Town is a vibrant place. There are pristine mountain reserves and long white beaches. There's a rhythm that pulses from the ground, an energy that can put a spring in your step, if you let it.

I had taken the slow way to the top of Table Mountain, using the steep footpath that climbed beneath the wires of the cable-car. That way, when I emerged on the dramatic plateau, I felt that I had earned the view.

The town itself was nestled below the mountain. A thousand metres below me, the sea crashed against the rocky coastline. From Cape Point to Cape Town, the same backbone of mountains weaves like a serpent, creating bays to the west and protected lands to the east. And out in the flats, the crunch and grind of construction continued as Cape Town grew. Houses were built to replace the large shanty-towns, yet the shanties just sprang up in new places, reusing the same cast-off building materials. Like some amateur environmental project, the city recycled itself.

Table Bay curved away from me, beyond the harbour, beyond the housing developments and away into the distance. Farmlands marked out the horizon with gold, green and brown, and beyond the industry and houses, I could see the twisted line of the Hottentots' Holland Mountains. As soon as I saw them, I knew that it wasn't the city I had come back for, it was for those mountains that I was in the west.

I was here to fly, to find the answers, to find myself.

# FLYING ALONE

11:40, Thursday : "I'm going bivouac flying," I shouted across to one of the pilots who had joined me on the hill. I packed a can of sweetcorn into my harness for effect.

"What's that?" he responded, playing along.

"I'll take off from here, fly to the mountains and sleep in the peaks somewhere tonight. Then tomorrow I'll just find another launch site and keep flying. I want to see how far I can get using only my feet and the glider." I pretended that I considered this flight possible. From an eighty-metre-high training hill.

"Great, then we won't have to worry about following you with your car," my friend replied, with a sly grin.

"Just leave it here and I'll pick it up when I return to Cape Town," I replied. I laughed, pulled up my glider and ran off the slope into the air.

\* \* \*

12:00, Thursday : I banked over hard, once again tracking across the gentle slope to try and gain some height. The lift was weak, and the slope wasn't very promising. It was used by student pilots during their training due to three facts; it had a very gradual slope, it was covered with soft vegetation and it was not very high. This produced mild conditions with no hazards apart from the ground itself. And no strong thermals. It was a short walk back to the top at the end of a flight, a walk which I was considering, sinking lower and lower over the scrub.

I glanced back toward the spectators on the crest of the hill; the students, the instructors and the merry hangers-on. They were all watching me. They probably expected me to magically discover some huge thermal, go kapow! into the sky and disappear.

I sank even lower. A friend glided past and ventured out over the fields to my left.

Poor lad, I thought. There would be no lift over there.

We had come to this little hill in desperation - nowhere else was flyable due to the strong wind. There's a meteorological effect called wind gradient which means that the lower you are the less wind you encounter, so we figured we would escape the wind by picking the smallest hill in the area. There was little chance of going cross country from there, we had just planned to float around a bit to appease the flying hunger.

The glider that had passed me began to climb, out over the fields.

It would be a tiny puff of lift, it would soon die.

The glider climbed and climbed, flying straight out away from the hill and rising rapidly into the blue sky. I cursed my dumb negativity. How many times did I need to learn the same lesson?

Expect a miracle!

I joined my friend in the widest, largest thermal I have ever seen at the training site and we circled gaily up and away. From the ground it must have looked like we had magically discovered a huge thermal, gone kapow! into the sky and disappeared. Just like that.

There was a thrill in leaving the ground behind and setting off on an adventure. I turned and turned in the thermal, drifting behind the hill and over the wheat-fields of the coastal plains beyond.

\* \* \*

14:00, Thursday : At last, I had reached the mountains! Forty kilometres of slow, calculated flying over the wheat-fields had brought me to the barrier. The peaks towered above me as I carved into a thermal low down amongst the foothills.

Wham! I lost half my wing in a violent blast of turbulence.

I cursed and corrected the wing. The thermal continued to buck and twist beneath me, making for a wild ride, but it was going up so I held on.

Such a contrast to the flying over the flatlands! Out in the plains the wide, gentle thermals had risen sedately from the fields in giant columns, forming chubby cumulus clouds, the glider-pilot's friend, the cherub of the thermic sky. I had played leap-frog above the cloud-shadows, trying to predict which cloud would be building next, which thermal column to glide across to. Each cloud lasted for only ten or fifteen minutes, then they frayed and dissolved. But another would always form somewhere nearby.

Fffrrip! My wing opened from another deflation, jolting me out of my reverie. I kept turning in the same boisterous thermal. Finally I climbed out above the peaks. I began to relax as I put more and more height between me and the ground. Whizzing past jagged rocks in my canvas-and-foam harness always made me feel exposed; I prefered to be high. Being a bird meant altitude, as far as I was concerned. I wanted to be an eagle, not a turkey.

With the wind at my back, it made sense to fly north. The mountains beckoned with the allure of a long cross-country flight. If I could endure the turbulence and work the thermals I might even make it to the Dasklip Pass.

Such a flight would be over one hundred kilometres.

Highly unlikely. Better not think about it. Just fly.

\* \* \*

16:00, Thursday : I waved to the spectators on the Dasklip Pass. The pilots were packing up their equipment. The wind had become too strong and it was not flyable. The spectators waved back at me, puzzled. Where had I come from? I circled a few times in front of the Pass, gaining height. Then I sped off along the ridge.

The sun began to sink in the dusty afternoon sky. Although the wind had increased, the lift was diminishing rapidly as the heat faded from the brown fields beneath me. I was not going to be able to fly much further.

I could probably make it to the pass, a distant curve of road further north. I might have to stay there overnight; wait for the stronger thermals of the next day to boost me over the mountain chain and on, over the town of Citrusdal.

Maybe, if I was very lucky, I might be able to sneak over the mountains before the sun set and glide down to Citrusdal in one flight. It would make a wonderful stop-over; it was a quiet and friendly town amongst the citrus farmlands. But it was still far away.

\* \* \*

02:00, Friday : The cold night air tickled my nose and I sneezed. My woollen cap fell from my head. I picked it up from the wooden boarding. My glider rustled as I moved within it, crinkling into an even flatter bed than before. It was a decent sleeping bag, air-tight and so quite warm, and the sports stadium I had found was nicely sheltered. I snuggled down in my glider again. There were still a few hours before dawn.

I could see the dark shapes of houses and trees beneath the dim starry sky. The town of Citrusdal was quiet, a small village amidst the silent farmlands, the epitome of the peaceful country life. It was the end of yesterday's epic flight; a place to fill up on supplies, to enjoy an evening meal and some company.

And behind the town, off to the east, loomed a big peak called Duiwelskop which I suspected would make a great launchsite for the coming day. I could fly off Duiwelskop and soar on into the Cedarberg Range, fly north towards the desert. The peak was quite close to town. Shouldn't be more than a couple of hours of hiking, I thought. I was sure to find a path somewhere on it.

I smiled dreamily. Visions of flying high above the Cedarberg filled my mind as I rested my head on my harness and drifted back to sleep.

\* \* \*

09:00, Friday : After two hours of walking I had reached the second row of foothills. I sat down heavily on a smooth, shaded rock and allowed my pack to fall off my shoulders. I had set out early, at the crack of dawn, but it was already hot. A sheen of sweat covered my body. I stowed my T-shirt in a side pocket. I downed my Coke. When I had quenched my thirst there was less than a litre left. I was going to have to ration my drinking stops more severely if I wanted to succeed in ascending the peak in time to fly. I glanced up towards the summit and my heart sank. It still seemed too distant, too inaccessible.

After two hours I had only reached the base of this daunting mountain. I had lost the path in the tumble of rocks and hills.

I felt better after my rest in the shade. It was great to be released from the weight of my backpack. A grasshopper zizzed by and crash-landed into a bush.

"Flights in logbook, 823, number of crashes, 823," I said.

The grasshopper emitted a "brrreeeppp!" in my general direction, rubbing its hind legs vigorously as if protesting. Then it leapt into the air in a mad frenzy of beating wings and zizzed off, out of sight. I heard it crash a few seconds later and laughed. If I had to land like that on every flight I'd be a right mess by now.

The sun was eating into the shade. I shouldered my heavy pack again. The peak was daunting, but there was only one way of reaching a goal and that was to keep going towards it. Keep moving.

"Onwards and upwards," I instructed my pack, and it rode me hard toward the peak.

\* \* \*

12:00, Friday : The last few hours had been murderous. I had pushed through chest-high vegetation that clawed at my legs and clutched at my pack, threatening to drag me off-balance and tumble me back down the steep, rock-strewn slope.

Every new variation of spiky fynbos devised its own method of slowing my pace and straining my breathing. One low plant specialised in cracking into little pieces when stepped upon, which unbalanced me every time. Then there were the thorny creeper-like bushes which had a habit of hooking into my aching legs. Most of the other plants were simply in the way. They clung to plants on either side and refused to part. I had to climb over these tangled clumps, and my strength waned under the merciless midday sun.

I had to push on, I had to climb higher, for there was nowhere to launch down below; only further up the slope, closer to the burning sun did the vegetation relent and offer a few bare, rocky patches to lure me on. One large slab of rock glistened wetly. Maybe I'd find some water there. My drinking supply had already run dry. I'd started with two litres of Coca-Cola. It was now an empty bottle tied to the side of my pack. I had to push on, to climb up towards the peak, towards the launch site. Towards the sun.

\* \* \*

13:00, Friday : I had reached the heart of the adventure. I stood alone, on the surly peak of *Duiwelskop*, the Devil's Head, a mighty outpost of rock on the edge of the Cedarberg. The mountains spread out across the world from there, tangling in sharp, high curves to the north, clashing in sudden twists of cliffs that fell hundreds of metres to hidden valleys below to the south. I breathed in deeply, filling my lungs with the clear air. The wind whispered past me, carrying with it the vast silence that was created by the presence of so many mighty peaks, a silence that was of the mountains.

There was something in the silence, like hearing the roar of the oceans inside a seashell held to the ear. I had done that once and a vision had come to me, of a galleon sailing across a sparkling bay, white sails snapping taut on the masts, the sailors shouting to each other as they coiled rope on the deck. I could smell the salt and the wood, and I could hear the chuckle of water against the hull beneath me. All that, from the silence.

In the same way, I listened to the whispering wind, and I was gripped by the majesty of the ancient force that had created these mountains, a force that had not left this area, but was poised in the earth beneath the peaks themselves, waiting in restless patience, arching up towards the sky.

The peaks of the Cedarberg were like proud warriors, linked together into one presence, and I stood on their border atop Duiwelskop. Listening to the silence I could sense the tension. There was a barely audible hum, so deep that I wondered if I was thinking the sounds rather than hearing them.

I glanced around, feeling the awareness of the mountains focusing on me as the hum grew stronger. Then I heard a sharp crack and saw a huge boulder tumbling down a cliff, asteroids of stone spinning in its wake. But it was not falling anywhere near me; it was in my vision that I could watch the tumbling boulder, in the internal picture of the entire Cedarberg range. I was humbled by the scale of the rock around me.

\* \* \*

13:30, Friday : It was critical to launch at precisely the correct instant, for if I mistimed it I could be gliding down in sinking air all the way to the fields at the base of Duiwelskop, five-hundred metres below. The same fields that I had walked through, on my way up. I would have to begin the tough ascent all over again and would reach the launchsite late in the afternoon. If I reached it at all.

I pushed these thoughts out of my mind, focusing on the success of a perfect launch and climb-out. The alternative was not even worth thinking about, it was not a possibility. At half past one on a hot summer's day in the middle of the Cedarberg it just had to be flyable.

I was going to take off and circle skywards in strong thermals. This had to be true. I was going up! I could imagine myself carving huge turns in my first boisterous thermal, feeling gleeful.

With this visualised future in mind, I was surprised that there was no wind. I stood for ten minutes, clipped in and ready to fly.

The sun beat down and cooked me in my jacket and jeans. Sure, I'd need the windproof protection for the long, high flight, but it was murder on the ground. The temperature was rising, the heat pushed into the shadows, filling in beneath the bushes. Yet still there was no wind. There should be thermals bubbling off the plains far below, pulling upwards through the bushes, rushing towards the peaks.

Sweat ran down my forehead and collected behind my sunglasses, blurring my vision.

It was quiet.

\* \* \*

13:40, Friday : The thermal was upon me. Bushes shook, woken from their stupor. I could feel the hot air rushing past me, curling over the rocks, pushing up towards the peak. The core of the thermal would still be coming - a strong thrust that would tear up the slope in turbulent gusts, too wild to launch in. If I was going to take off, I had to go. No time to waste.

I pulled firmly on my glider and tried to keep it rising straight above my head, but it canted over to one side, buckling in the variable wind. I had little room to move; to my sides there were large boulders and a burnt tree, behind me a tangle of bushes and the steep mountain-slope. I had to guide my wing to lift me away from the dangers.

It began to drop back down. I coaxed the wing up, using all my skill just to keep the glider out of the scrub. It dropped back again, and a few lines caught around the rock, trapping half the wing. The wind rose at my back, I could sense the urgency of the thermal core only seconds away, approaching up the slope.

There was no-one else there, to pull my wing free, which is what I sorely needed. If I let the wing drop completely and gave up, it would take ages in the heat to untangle it and lay the wing out again.

I tried to extend myself into the wing, tried to sense things through the wing, as if it was part of my body. The wing twisted and buckled in the wind, its lines trapped. It felt as if my body was twisting and buckling. I could feel the air rushing about me, pushing into my brightly coloured fabric.

I surged forwards with a lively air current, pulling my lines tight around the rock. I knew how I could free myself, how I could open and release, soar out into the sky. I waited for the next lively gust and twisted away from the rock. Once my lines were taut once again I buckled back towards the snare, shooting past the rock and allowing my lines to droop loosely beneath me. I could see my human form standing below, balancing on two legs, tugging with two hands, unified with me, but I was the wing itself.

My lines went slack and slid off the rock. I flexed as the wind caught my liberated fabric, and I opened with a shock. I was lifting, surging forwards, plucking my human form off the slope with the talons of my harness.

We rushed outwards, as one form, into the most boisterous, violent thermal core that I have experienced for years. I didn't circle skywards, I rocketed towards the heavens, with a wild, wide grin.

I was flying.

\* \* \*

15:00, Friday : I surveyed the kingdom from my place of power, high in the sky. The Cedarberg Range crouched below me to the east, and far beneath my feet was the deep blue jewel of the Clanwilliam Dam. Without close reference points, my movement seemed majestic, a sedate glide over the tapestry of farmlands.

I looked into the hazy distance to the north. I could follow the line of ridges into unknown territory. Or I could cross the dwindling Cedarberg Mountains and venture into the Ceres-Karoo, a wasteland of scrub, rocks and sand.

Wherever I flew to, I would be alone.

I had decided to leave the roads behind. I wanted to find true freedom. In the early days I had needed friends around me when I flew, so that if something went wrong they would be there to help me. I followed the roads, and stuck to the known and safe. It was too risky to go out on my own in the beginning, because flying cross country can take you into some wild, exposed places. Luckily the leap from novice to cross-country pilot can be done in little steps.

The danger with the little steps is that they can become so small that you forget to keep moving.

So I had finally discarded the comfort of following the roads. I was completely alone, and at last I understood how liberating that was. I could go anywhere, do anything. There were no commitments to go to a certain place, to fly in a certain way; I was free to fly.

Anywhere.

Where would I land? How far would I have to walk out to reach civilisation? It didn't matter. There was nowhere I was trying to get back to. Instead, I was looking for lifting air currents, where the biggest mountains were. Where was the most exhilarating part of sky?

When a sword is dangled over our heads we discover surprising skills that we did not know we possessed. The risk of being completely alone in the sky formed that sharpened sword above my head. And so, my flying was transformed. I flew further, faster, with more confidence. To attain this freedom I had given up my need for security.

Having pulled away the safety net I walked a tightrope high above the earth. Every step counted, every step was filled with meaning. I had to perform impeccably.

I was alone and free. I glided on, over Clanwilliam Dam, heading for the distant mountains.

\* \* \*

16:00, Friday : I entered a wide valley of tended fields. A ridge ran along its eastern border. I marvelled at the perfect geometry, a slope created by two angles of rock. The lower slopes ran smoothly up from the fields. The cliffs that capped the ridge were vertical and of uniform height. It looked as if some Giant had taken a builder's trowel to the landscapes and carved an edge to the flat plateau.

As I glided over to the eastern ridge, the warm air of the valley surrounded my wing in buoyant, gentle currents. The valley exuded a sense of peace, a mood of patience and slow growth. Across the valley the western hills were folded softly about their afternoon shadows like resting lions. Their rumps caught the sun, rich browns and ochres in the light, their forepaws stretched out languidly into the dusty green and tan of the fields.

A truck moved along a road in the distance, tossing a trail of dust into the air. I became absorbed in the geometry of everything in the valley. The dust drifted away in the wind, forming a line on the north side of the road, creating a wedge design, with the truck at the apex of the wedge. A field created a third line in the distance to make a triangle. Fences divided the ground into octagons, hexagons, rectangles. The canal and road, far away, formed parallel lines below the third parallel of the horizon. My wing arced smoothly above me, next to the sinking circle of the sun. Out in the fields there were two perfect circles, scribed by the rotation of large irrigation systems. They were coloured a rich green in their centre, and tracks radiated from them like the extended spokes of a wheel.

It was a joy to be floating along that ridge. The wind pushed steadily against the cliffs, providing a consistent band of lift. I didn't need to turn or do anything. I could merely point my glider down the ridge, and fly north. Everything seemed surreal.

I had entered another world.

\* \* \*

17:00, Friday : Suddenly, beside me, was an eagle, gliding on silent wings. A tawny-feathered bird, with a rounded tail, yellow eyes wide in curiosity, wings trimmed back to remain alongside my imperfect craft. I love the way birds can move their necks with such flexibility, twisting their heads about to get a better view while their wings remain locked in steady glide. The eagle treated me to a contortionist's demonstration.

[Your wings make me laugh too. Good to fly with you, Skywalker.]

The thought was like a clear voice, loud and undeniable. There weren't words, but I interpreted them as such; I encountered the *idea* of the words. From the bird? Maybe Beagle had been telling the truth after all. I wondered where he was, at that moment. What had he said? That they had a piercing way of passing their thoughts on to their kind. Maybe if the eagle had just ordained to 'speak' to me, then it would be prepared to at least try to listen to my response.

It had called me Skywalker.

Was that because I flew with my legs down? Or had it seen me walking up the mountain? How did I get to speak like that? And if I could, what could I ask it about? The brown-feathered beauty of the skies must know a thousand things about flying, things I could learn.

But if I just flew with the bird, I could pick up all these secrets practically. It would be a waste of a question. What on earth do you ask an eagle when it has just spoken to you?

I tried to greet the eagle in kind, asking for its name.

[tangle of forests] came the reply. I had the feeling that it wasn't answering my question; it was a general comment.

[your mind / tangle of forests / I cannot see]

I got it that time. Beagle had said something similar about our thoughts. It shouldn't stop me from trying, I thought. If I was successful and could talk to that eagle, what would I learn? I wondered if it was male or female. I wondered how you tell them apart. Probably female, they were usually smaller. I wondered why I couldn't stop my mind from firing off so many questions. I tried to think clearly of what I wanted.

[less tangle, same forest] the eagle seemed to say.

I was going to have to do better. I relaxed, meditated, calming my bubbling internal dialogue. I focused on one word at a time.

"Hello.what.is.your.name?"

[sundancer]

Sundancer! She had answered my question!

I rejoiced. I had communicated with an eagle. Where could I go from here, what secrets could I uncover? What did Sundancer believe in, what was her mission, what did eagles do high up there above the peaks, when the hunting was far below? Would she stay beside me in the air for long? What did it feel like to strike a mouse?

[speak in silence] she said, and then [i tire]

The eagle's parting cry rang out with a strangely musical quality, as if it contained a melody. Had they always sounded like that, or was it just this eagle? Had my hearing changed, was I able to perceive more within the apparent simplicity of my reality?

I received no answer to my many questions, for the eagle had gone, and I was left to glide on toward the golden sun alone.

I felt a pang of loss. I had botched a perfect opportunity, wasted my first contact with an eagle because of the racing of my mind. Yet I was inspired. There was a new magic in my world, and I was determined to pursue it.

Mental silence - that had been Beagle's problem as well.

\* \* \*

18:00, Friday : I had reached the end of the ridge. The sun was setting, the wind pushing me out over the plains, away from the lifting air, into a wilderness where the wind blew straight and strong, offering no assistance to me and my drifting, sinking wing. I glided over the dusty land trying to cover as much ground as possible before my inevitable landing. I gazed ahead trying to judge how far I would go, when I saw a strip of tarred road running along the base of the hills. Now that I had rounded the corner of the plateau I could discern the dark line in the light brown of the desert.

I wriggled in my harness. It was going to be an easy walk. I could hitch-hike home! I had flown without concern for the roads, I had been prepared to walk out from wherever. But there it was, a highway, running straight across my flightpath. It was time to graciously retire. I glided out, and touched down in the windy open expanse beside the black line that led back to civilisation.

It was two-hundred-and-fifty kilometres back to my car, where I had left it the day before atop a small hill on the coastal plain outside Cape Town. I hummed a song as I walked to the nearby town. I watched the gathering dusk. I felt at home.

It had taken me many years to finally master my fear of being completely alone in the sky. Many small steps taken in the same direction had eventually covered the distance. The world had finally opened up to me.

I was free.

# A HEAD IN THE CLOUDS

Some days are just made for flying. Perfect little cumulus clouds whiffling in a deep blue sky, cold, crisp air aloft and a fiery sun baking the ground. If you could package this weather in a can it would be labelled 'Perfect Sky, just add water.' You'd be a millionaire in a week. Every glider pilot the world over would move heaven and earth to buy some stock.

On this particular Saturday, I really needed a can or two of Perfect Sky. I was faced with the weather that would have been left out of the can. A fine blanket of high cirrus cloud shrouded the sun from a thicker layer of low stratus that drifted about indecisively. The wind was light and variable.

I piled into my car and rushed off to my favourite flying site, one hundred kilometres away. I had nothing better to do.

It was a week since I had been in the Cedarberg and I was missing the mountains already. Cape Town had provided me with some gentle soaring over great scenery, but the ease of city-living was already wrapping its treacherous vines about my ankles. I needed to get free, to feel the cold, high wind blowing through me, to be cleansed by the deprivation of hiking in the wilderness.

"It's on days like these that you often have incredible flights," my friend chirped from the back seat. Peering over the pile of gliders and squinting out at the landscape rushing by, he was the picture of enthusiasm. Flying peak-cap jammed firmly over unkempt hair, sunglasses in place, heavy-duty boots on his restless feet. He was going flying, come hell or high water, no matter what the weather-office said.

"What happens is that you don't expect anything great, and the day, well, it surprises you and becomes flyable," he added. "Even a bit of airtime becomes a little miracle!"

Travelling with optimists is good for the soul.

The flying site was far away, and must have different weather, we decided. So by default it was good, because where we were wasn't good. Was it getting clearer up ahead, wasn't that a patch of sun?

Soon we reached the launch site. We swung the car doors open. It looked flyable! Although clouds blanketted the sky, the wind was blowing gently up the mountain. We carried our gliders up to the launch area and soon we were airborne, with fresh mountain air rushing past our helmets, through our lines and under our feet.

Big flights always sneak up on me. They begin with a few innocent thermals, and I work each one, slowly gaining height, turn after turn, as the world drifts by below. Before I know it, the cross-country adventure has begun.

Another thermal bumped my glider skywards. I turned, and turned again in lazy circles. I glided on to the next sunny slope. I glanced back toward the launch site to check my position. The launch site! It had disappeared in a haze of distance.

My friend flew with me for a while, but he chose a different route away from the mountains and vanished. I was left alone in a huge sky.

I climbed up the windward face of Saron Peak, thermalling from low down amongst the rocks. The rockfaces were dramatic, with sharp tentacles of rock jutting upward towards me, reaching out from the recesses of a mountain that rose one thousand metres. The uneven surface twisted the wind into strange currents. Being wary of the cliffs, I kept my distance, banking in wide circles until finally I rose above the highest peak. As I glided south, I enjoyed the view of the valley exposed behind the peaks. I had hoped to climb higher, but it was important to cover distance. Being just past noon, the thermals should have been in their prime, but they were still weak.

The mountains drop down to a low set of ridges to the south of Saron Peak and I found myself scratching around close to the ground in a strong north-westerly wind. I began to drift backwards over the ridges with every turn. The wind pushed me towards a narrow pass that cut through the hills. I beat across the wind and scuttled off further south.

Massive peaks towered into the clouds in the distance, their faces carved by the passage of time. The clouds were dark and hungry-looking. I couldn't gauge how high the clouds extended above the peaks, for I was looking at them from below. Rain coursed down in the distance.

There was not another soul in the sky. No aeroplanes, no birds, not even a tractor chugging across the ground far below to break the solitude. I was alone and free in my newly mastered realm.

The wind drew patterns on the large dam below me. Twists and curls developed on the water-surface, dervishes that chased and tumbled over each other until they reached the leeward bank and whisked into the protection of the forests. The trees formed a dense plantation that stretched around the dam and onto the foothills beneath me. Tucked away in the forest were two houses, idyllic looking retreats.

I was blown further south by the freshening wind.

The ground became flat and featureless beneath me. No farms, no roads, no trees. The nearest activity was some traffic far out in the valley on the road to Wellington. A very unlucky-looking place to land.

Suddenly my variometer began to scream. The air was going up! No, not just up. Up Very Fast. Dark, misty tendrils groped down from the gunmetal-grey clouds and pulled at my glider. If this lift continued, it would take me into the darkness, into the cold, wet dangerous haze. I'd be unable to see where the looming peaks were.

I collapsed my wingtips, hoping to sink downwards. I went up.

The horizon began to disappear in the mists. I banked my glider into a spiral and held on. My wing speeded up, the wind whistled in my ears, but the ground disappeared.

There was cloud all around me. I lent deeper and deeper into the spiral. The world was spinning but I couldn't see anything. My harness creaked. The wind tore past my face.

Then things got strange. The wind quietened. I was wrapped in an ominous hush. The grey was oppressive, pushing in toward me from all sides; undefined, unshaped. I couldn't see further than the end of my arm.

There were no reference points, nothing to hold onto.

I suppose that is how a deceased spirit feels when rising into the spiritual world. Without feedback from my senses, my image of the world began to crumble and dissolve, leaving me disorientated and fearful, unsure of how to place myself in a world with no reference points.

I looked upwards in the grey, where I thought Up should be, to find the sun. There was only a diffused glow that came from everywhere in the mist around me. I stretched out my hand to create a shadow to deduce the sun's position, but there was no shadow in the moist fog. I gazed around, hopelessly lost. Mist, haze, damp and fog. I didn't even know which way was up.

A dark shape hurtled through the cloud and paused in front of me. For an unbearable second it seemed that a huge Being was looking at me. My heart beat frantically.

I didn't want to know what it was, I didn't want to see. I dived my glider deeper into the spiral, dived from the dark dread face of cold mist, dived until the tears streamed from my eyes in the fierce rush of wind and my stomach rolled in agony at the force. I began to lose consciousness as my vision reduced to a tunnel of grey before me. I could hear a cacophony of sounds as my ears struggled in the pressure - the sounds of children laughing, but warped as if played backwards on a stretched tape, the hubbub of an airport terminal, arguing voices, screeching cats and distressed chickens, all sampled together. The soundtrack to my own horror movie.

A face in the cloud? I couldn't be sure, it wasn't there any more. Maybe it had been a reflection of the peaks, or some large bird.

Suddenly I had a moment of clarity.

I had just seen my fear. The face was just a reflection of what was going on in my mind, my panic, my dreadful fear. Hadn't I thought about breaking through the clouds only a few weeks ago? Didn't they represent my greatest fear, that of losing my sight?

I had already made a decision on clouds, already decided to bust through the vaporous illusion of this fear. I should be ready for the test.

The fact that I was beneath a big, dark grey brooding cloud was not simply a consequence of random chance. I had moved myself into that position through my choice to fly that specific route, at that specific time. I had been in a position to choose my direction. Call it the guiding hand of intuition, call it Fate, what you will. I was not being preyed on by a cloud. I had preyed on myself with a cloud. It was my test, a challenge to prove my mastery.

If I spiralled out of the cloud in fear, I would fail.

I thought back to the wild meerkat-monster in the forest, and my scampering up the 'avalanche' with Beagle laughing from above. I recalled the moment when I'd leapt beyond my fear of losing control, when I'd jumped from the waterfall.

I levelled out of the spiral, and faced my fear.

A part of me was still terrified. A small voice chittered nervously in my head, assuring me that I was crazy, that this was insane, I did not want to do this, I would get hurt, I would die. I thanked my fear for telling me that I was scared. But now I knew that there was something beyond the fear, something worth pursuing.

The cloud swallowed me in its angry belly. It twisted and roared around my wing, tossing me about as if I were a toy. I held on grimly and tried to centre on a strong lifting current that would pull me upwards, higher into the cloud and away from the danger of the concealed peaks.

After a few turns I had completely lost my sense of direction. Everything was grey. I could see that my one brake was engaged, which should induce a turn in the glider, but I couldn't feel it. I had to assume that I was turning. Sight was more important than I had thought.

In the complete greyness of surrounding moisture, I found the shift into using the Eagle's perspective almost natural. I needed to know where I was. The urgency sharpened my perception. I ventured out and away from my body, searching down through the vaulted tumble of cloud for the danger of the mountain peak.

Everything was grey, a damp confusion of cloying wetness. I pushed further out with my mind. I was determined to find some direction in the sea of uncertainty. Slowly I began to sense the wet rocks of the cliffs, far behind and below me. I could make out the vague shape of the ridge hidden in the curling base of the cloud. I turned to fly in a direct line away from the cliffs, directly out to the west.

Water sprayed over me. I looked up. My lines extended from my carabiners to the wing eight metres above. Along each line, drops of water collected. I had become a giant spider, sitting at the centre of my web. The droplets ran down the lines and fed the spider, who sat waiting in the centre of the web.

Except that this spider wasn't particularly thirsty.

I was soaked within seconds. Water ran across my chest and dribbled off into the passing wind. I hoped that I would burst through the side of the cloud into the sunshine soon. I was growing cold. I suppose spiders pack up their webs when it rains. Or they stay indoors.

The grey continued. Formless, thick, monotonous grey. Although I had an idea of where the mountains were now, the scene lacked the sensual enjoyment that landscapes normally bring to me from the air. I grew bored of being a wet spider staring at a grey wall.

Maybe the Buddha could stare at the brick wall of his cell for six months and gain enlightenment, but I would need to find another way, I would go mad first.

*Patience. Quiet. Silence.*

My patience was wearing thin, the quiet was beginning to become oppressive, and if the silence didn't shut up, I was going to scream. Clouds are effective isolation chambers. I wanted out.

Pow! I burst out through the western edge of the towering cumulus, high above the plains, cold and dazzled by the bright sunshine and stupendous view.

The world was filled with such intensity I was overwhelmed. Such colours! Such beautiful forms! I could not remember it being so rich in every sense, so vital. The vast empty lands below, with trees! and rocks! and hills, valleys, rivers, roads, sunlight! oh glorious light! here, and there, far in the distance, touching the plains.

It was a different world to the one I'd left before the cloud. There was so much to see, I absorbed imagery like a thirsty sponge. I saw the way the farms blended into each other, fences vague in the distance. A fence was something you'd only see well if you were short-sighted; from up in the sky I could see forever. I could perceive the health of the land below me, the energy of vital, growing things. This vitality linked the vegetation. The ground pulsed with goodness, with well-being. I looked down at the face of my world and I loved it. It was beautiful.

I floated on, in silence.

Flying conditions weakened as the afternoon wore on. I flew through gentle thermals and larger expanses of still air. I sank lower and lower, like a large, heavy bird hugging the contours of the cliffs, and then the slopes, then the foothills. I breathed in on every turn, as if to make my body lighter. I visualised myself floating. I was a balloon. I was weightless.

The clouds in the distance opened up, and the sun, in flaming glory, burst through. Shafts of light streamed through the gaps like sand pouring through many fingers. The trees, the paths, the fields and fences, the dark brown earth, everything basked in the golden light. And ahead of me, in a sunny gorge, I could see the beginnings of a new thermal forming. Leaves and dust whirled up from the ground, and a cluster of swallows were skimming in and out of the debris, darting this way and that to hunt down disturbed insects. I rode it as high as I could, up to the peaks.

The sunlight touched the dams that lay beneath me in the farmlands. The water sparkled for a while, then the wind calmed altogether, and the dams lay as smooth as glass.

The mountains stood out in dramatic clarity, each proud, gigantic peak depicted in folded shadow and light. There was a chiselled face of grey beside me which thrust out into the valley. Beyond it were darker, deeper cliffs of silver. Behind those, towering in the background, stood the older peaks, a weathered grey-blue. These mountains had been born aeons before mankind and would live long into the future. I flew past them, taking a moment of their eternal beauty for my own.

As the sun sank into the distant horizon, I glided out over the fields. I seemed to fly forever, with the smooth air holding my wing, and the ground drifting under my feet. But at last the sun set, leaving me to start a new day in another land, and the spell was broken. Earth crunched beneath my feet as I touched down in a darkening field of cooling air.

I was transformed.

I was far, far away from where I had begun on that dreary morning. It is on days like these that you can have your best flights.

# RETURN TO MAGIC

As the cool night wrapped around the fading mountains, I reached the picturesque town of Franschhoek on foot. Franschhoek had been established as a settlement for the French Huguenots centuries ago, and since then the farmlands had been lovingly tended. Many hands over many years had smoothed out every imperfection, leaving the land clean and smooth, the vineyards in neat rows, the grass trimmed short. But every here and there the defiant South African wilderness pushed through the surface, with a clump of shrubs here, a wild forest, a patch of proteas. Beyond the town, the slopes bristled with fynbos.

The warm light from a small restaurant spilled onto the sidewalk, drawing me in. 'Le Coq au Vin' seemed like the perfect place to stop off for the night; it seemed to have rooms as well. Cutlery clanked and glasses clinked. The scent of good food wafted out from the doorway. I had an intuitive feeling that this was the right place to be.

The host was a portly man in a green waistcoat, who waggled about like a duck. He put his guests at ease with light jests, moving from table to table. Every patron received his attention, every one was appraised with the same charm. Finally he bore down on the front desk.

"Good evening, good evening! I'm Frederique. My my my - you've brought your whole house with you!"

I felt my paraglider cringe in its bag. It was an elegant restaurant.

"Sorry, it's my paraglider," I explained, "is there somewhere I can put it? I'd like to stay for the night, if you have a room available."

"Certainly, certainly!" He appraised me with beady eyes. "You'll be wanting a shower as well then," he asserted, as if to say, I shouldn't really return without one. "I'll call Alicia down, she'll show you your room." He squashed a little red button on the desk. A bell tinkled in the background.

My room was cosy. A thick blue carpet and cream curtains. En-suite bathroom. I dumped my paraglider on the floor. Ah, it was good to let the weight fall off my back.

The evening was going to be expensive, but every once in a while it's good to treat yourself. It recharges your enthusiasm for those long mountain ascents. I stepped into the shower and let the dust and grime of the day wash off my body.

Back in the restaurant, I ordered myself a fresh garlic bread and soup. Once I had started on it, Frederique waddled over to give me the inspection.

"How is the soup?" he asked.

"Myngh, mff." I nodded, enthusiastically. Why did they always do that? The question always came when your mouth was full.

A gentle music began to play, filling the gaps in conversations. It added romance to the room. Frederique had chosen well; the flute was being played perfectly. I almost recognised the piece - a high melody supported on a lower structure - not Beethoven, more modern ...

When I saw who was playing the flute, just inside the door of the restaurant, I almost choked on the mouthful of bread I was chewing.

His dark hair in a wild chaos on his shoulders, his strong hands running lightly over the flute, working the music out of the silver instrument with concentrated passion. Beagle.

I jumped to my feet and spilled soup on the table. Blast! It would have to wait. I strode across the restaurant to greet my friend.

"Bartholomew the Bard at your service," he said, bending at the waist when he had finished his tune.

"Wonderful to see you!" I welcomed him. "What brings you here?" The last I had seen of Beagle had been in the Drakensberg, walking away from the mountain-club hut down the road. That he should be here, at the same time as me, so distant from that sunny morning!

"A lone eagle often travels a long way before finding a friend."

"You're hoping to find eagles out here? I haven't seen any in Franschhoek, but I met a beauty in the Cedarberg a week ago."

"What was she called? Oh, you wouldn't know," he ended, downcast.

"Sundancer," I replied.

"Sundancer? Are you sure?" His face lit up. "She talked to you!"

"Well, yes, for a little while."

"Bless the Creator! Ah, that is a special bird." His eyes held a faraway gaze, remembering. "And you talked to her! My friend, you really are ready for the west!"

I was a little puzzled by his words. Ready for the west?

"Sundancer is a guide. She has had four partners that I know of. She leads initiates into the world beyond death."

I went cold. What was he saying? That she killed her mates?

Frederique had come bustling across. "Excuse me for interrupting, gentlemen! That music you were playing was most beautiful. Do you think we could have some more?" He waved a hand at his restaurant, at the people enjoying their meals.

"Certainly," Beagle responded, with a twinkle in his eye. "For a meal and a bed, I'll play until midnight."

Frederique continued to smile, but his eyes angled away as he calculated the value of the trade. "I would be honoured," he replied. "Can I offer you a drink to enjoy before you begin?"

"A wine from the area, something red, would be wonderful."

I led Beagle across to my table.

"Sundancer!" he exclaimed. "What a surprise, I haven't seen her for years, for she rarely emerges on this side of the barrier. I have been wanting to work with her since I first discovered what her mission was."

"The barrier?" This was new to me.

"The barrier, the separation between this plane and the next. Not so much a barrier as it is a different level of vibration, or frequency." He saw my puzzled expression. "There are different levels of reality, they exist at the same time in the same space, but you can only perceive the one plane that you are tuned in to. If you alter your frequency, other worlds become available to you. It's like many radio stations, all sharing the same air. Tune in to the right one, and your whole life can change. But it's not easy to shift, and most of the folk here are happy with the Consensus Reality show."

I picked at my garlic bread. As usual, Beagle was turning my known world upside down. A multi-layered reality with planes of vibration?

"Sundancer is a special one. She can teach others to shift beyond death to a separate reality, she can take them with her. For you to have seen her and spoken to her without observing anything else out of the ordinary means that she must have shifted down into this plane."

I was finding it hard to believe. "I can keep an open mind, but I have no experience of these other worlds."

"No experience!" Beagle was suddenly angry. "Stop lying to yourself! If you had no experience of shifting worlds, you'd still be in the city, wouldn't you?"

"That's not the same, is it?" I said in a small voice.

"You see the world differently, not so? You respond to your intuition. You wouldn't have met me if you couldn't shift, you are already in a different world."

"Why are you in my world?" I asked.

"Why are you in mine?" he responded. "Maybe we both need something from each other."

I wondered what Beagle could possibly need from me.

"You must have shifted from when I last met you. I left that world behind. You've moved fast. You didn't notice any change, recently? A colour shift, a deepening of beauty?"

At once I thought of coming out of the cloud. The world *had* seemed different, transformed, more alive. I had seen the vitality in the soil, shimmering into the trees, the energy pulsing beneath the land. Maybe that was another level of reality, a plane of visible health, that was overlaid on the ordinary world. Ever since then everything I'd seen had this shimmer of beauty. I'd put it down to being high from my great flight. But Beagle might be right, I might have already shifted planes.

He drained the last of his glass and stood up. "Excuse me while I entertain my keeper for my keep."

A few of the customers noticed him as he moved to the end of the room, and they fell silent in an expectant hush, nudging their companions. Beagle raised the flute to his lips, and gently introduced his music into the space.

My main course arrived with a flourish from Frederique, who appeared to hold me in higher esteem as the friend of an accomplished musician than as a paraglider pilot. I enjoyed my vegetable platter. The cooking was superb, and I had a healthy supply of hunger ladled on top of it.

Beagle began a song. There was no accompaniment, just his melodic voice, and yet he commanded such attention in the room.

*You want to know the reason why*
*my light has caught your roving eye*
*before the subtle shimmers die*
*you pull me down so I can't fly*

*Only to find it wasn't me*
*that I am not what I seem to be*
*I was different when I was free*
*where is my luminosity?*

*The more you try to see the light*
*the harder it will be to sight*
*you chase a butterfly so bright*
*how quickly it will fly in fright*

*There is something you should know*
*if you were a flower I wouldn't go*
*you'd have your own colours and inner glow*
*so let your soul shine and the magic will flow*

*I want to know the reason why*
*your light has caught my roving eye*
*before the subtle shimmers die*
*I join your side so we can fly.*

There was a round of applause as Beagle bowed. His magic lingered in the room. I reflected on Beagle's mastery - there were over fifty people in the restaurant, every one was paying for their meal, all except for Beagle. Slowly the conversations began again, and Beagle started a gentle melody on his flute. It was a soft trickling stream of sound with a mysterious rhythm.

Suddenly I could appreciate a new depth within the music. The poetry of it. The beauty. I was aware of the shift this time as the world deepened around me. A lightness of being filled me. I sensed the spaces between the notes in Beagle's music as if they were shapes. I looked at the little pot-plant standing beside my table, and I saw the spirit within its curving form. I could see an etheric field of energy outlining my fingers. I laughed, full of joy. I had a glimpse of enlightenment.

I knew at once that I would drop off the high soon and return to the duller reality. The awareness had come upon me like a rushing wind. I had never experienced such a shift before. I wanted to stay there, to feel so inspired. Why did I have to return to the dullness of normality, where my emotions were just shadows of what I could feel now?

I felt like kissing the woman across the room, a complete stranger. I wanted to share my experience of her sudden beauty with her. But I knew I would be misunderstood.

How could I express to others what it was that I perceived? I was like a cartoon character who had emerged from his two-dimensional world and had discovered the wonder of three dimensions. There were no adequate words to explain the liberation I felt. I only wished I could share it with others.

Beagle came across to sit at my table, accepting another glass of wine from Frederique on the way.

"What happened back there?" I asked.

"Where?" Beagle replied.

He was on his usual form, pretending complete innocence.

"With the music! There was something else happening besides notes on a flute. There was - an enlightenment."

"Ah, that. That had little to do with me."

"Then - what?"

"I created a doorway. An aperture. You were the one who stepped through it, as did that man in the far corner, and the woman in the green dress, beside the front desk." He motioned vaguely with his hand. The woman smiled at us. She was the pretty one I'd suddenly noticed before.

"To everyone else, it was just a nice little bit of flute music." He sipped on his red wine, savouring the taste before swallowing.

"You're saying there's a gateway one can use to shift to the next plane?" I was excited. This knowledge had eluded me for years. I'd had my moments of perspective, but they were random and infrequent.

He nodded, eyes a gleeful sparkle.

"Oh come on!" I said. "You're drawing me along. Tell me how it works."

"You sure you're not placing too much importance on this?"

"No. I mean yes!"

He laughed then, guessing how desperate I was to find the instant solution to my spiritual growth.

"You are the key," he said.

I was silent, absorbing what he said, turning it over and over in my mind.

"That's it?"

It was his turn to be silent now, smiling with an aloof gaze, enjoying my struggle.

I am the key. I am the key? What did that mean? It didn't help at all. I felt robbed, cheated of a promised knowledge. If I was the key to my enlightenment, then I would already be enlightened, wouldn't I? How could I use myself to unlock a door which I could not see?

"I can't explain the secret," Beagle said. "The real essence is that you are the key."

"The key to what?"

"To enlightenment. Look, I am a mystic, not a scientist, so I just use the magic. I don't scrutinise it's inner workings. But I do know that what we choose to pay attention to in this world determines what we experience. Think about it; again, it's like radio. Music is being beamed through your body right now without you being aware of it. Then you turn on the right kind of reception, and the sounds emerge. The experience of enlightenment comes about because you choose to see deeper into reality. You choose to hear music, so you do. The world is transformed for you because of your attention."

"And the gateway? How did you get us to shift?"

"It is simple for me to open the door. I was already there, I just expressed what I heard. I played something from the higher plane. Only a few of you sensed it. You were receptive. As I said, you are the key, I can't make you see."

"Why doesn't it last?" I asked, disappointed with myself.

"Sometimes it happens by accident, we feel and see the beauty for a few moments. Either way, when we shift down to normality, we forget. Unless we are in a state of enlightenment, we cannot appreciate the experience, we just have a vague recollection. We lose the vision. That's normal."

"But how do we hold onto the perspective? I always want to hear music in that way."

"You have to reach up, and continue to reach up."

I thought about this. So to be inspired by beauty one had to keep looking for it, and believe it was there even when you didn't see it. He was talking about faith.

"Are there more planes beyond the one you used?"

Beagle smiled. "There may be an infinity beyond."

"Where did you learn all this from?"

"I had good teachers. You met one of them already."

I looked at him blankly.

Beagle continued. "Remember Sundancer? She inhabits a powerful plane. In the same way that I might be able to guide you, she can guide me to transcend my current level and pass beyond death. She guided me years ago, but then she disappeared. That is the way with good teachers. They appear precisely when you are ready for what they have to teach."

He paused. "That's my cue," he said, and grinned like a wolf. He left me.

Although Beagle was set to play until midnight, I could not stay awake. The ordeal and ecstasy of my flight, the long walk into town and the intensity of Beagle's concepts had drained me. I made my excuses and turned in for the night. I had a lot to think about.

I had a lot to dream about.

# STEPS AHEAD

The crunch of vegetation measured out a steady, slow beat under my feet. The plan was to head north along the mountain chain, towards Porterville and the Cedarberg beyond. We had stocked up with some supplies in Franschhoek after breakfast, and were set for a good few days of hiking and flying in the wilderness. Beagle wanted to search for birds, I wanted to become one. The wind was blowing strongly from the east, so I resigned myself to a stiff hike, unable to fly in the prevailing conditions.

Beagle was silent, striding ahead along the hiking trail, gazing far ahead into the distant peaks.

My mind ticked over to the rhythm of our steady walking pace. At first I had tried to get Beagle to talk. I was full of questions. But slowly, over the hours of hiking, my mind began to clear, to slow down to the beat of my feet crunching in the gravel and rocks. Fewer and fewer thoughts skidded across the wide surface of my inner pool of quiet, each one leaving ever smaller ripples. The world reflected in the pool began to change, becoming somehow more real than before, more intense. I lifted my sunglasses from my head to see if it was just a trick of my eyes, or if the sun had emerged from some high cloud ...

The sky was a brilliant, rich blue above me, from horizon to horizon, not a cloud in sight. Something was different. Surely the sky had not been so blue before, so richly, wonderfully, immensely blue? The bushes, hadn't they been more drab and dusty beside the path, not always so green and bursting with life? Where had all those little insects come from, scurrying in vibrant activity amongst the leaves? The enhanced perspective had returned, no warning, no heraldic trumpets, I had simply fallen through the barrier once again, as clumsily as ever. I scanned my mind for clues to how the shift had been initiated.

It seemed to have something to do with the mental silence. When I wanted to perceive the magic beneath the surface of the world and I approached it in an intellectual fashion, willing my eyes to see more than what they were seeing, to hear more than I was hearing, my mind simply filled up with questions, observations and arguments that attempted to shoot down my strange beliefs in a hail of logic. As soon as my mind was filled with the normal chatter of thoughts, my old established reality was the only one in view.

When I just observed the world, in silence, without analysing or rationalising it, a greater picture began to emerge.

The flowers were not just colourful, they were brilliant, shining out from the protection of the scrub on both sides of the hiking path. The scents of fynbos filled my nostrils with a pungent fervour, rich with the spice of life. The earth pushed up underneath my feet and I could feel its rumpled form, warming in the healthy sunshine. The trees growing in a river-gully bristled with vitality, and I could hear them whispering to each other. The river chuckled along its bed, a musical synthesis of swirls and tumbles over the rocks in its path.

The river seemed to draw the impurity out of everything that surrounded it. It was more than just a course of water running downhill; it was a vein of healing, drawing the impure energy out of the land, dissolving the dis-eases, leaving the land pure and clean. All the vegetation that lived within its influence grew sturdy and beautiful, unmarred by darkened energy fields that some other plants demonstrated. I stopped beside the river, motioning to Beagle to continue, that I would catch up soon.

"Don't spend too long there," he cautioned. "Rivers clean, but they'll eventually drain your power if you're not careful on this level."

"Thanks, I'll just be a moment," I responded, waving him on and pulling off my boots to sink my feet into the coolness. A shiver of pleasure ran down my spine as my skin touched the water.

Rivers don't normally feel so good, I thought to myself. Was this energy only coming to me because I had begun to perceive its resonance, tuned in to a different station, so to speak? The tiredness in my muscles and joints dissolved; it was sucked away by the river's healing current.

\* \* \*

We camped high in the mountains that night, overlooking the town of Paarl. From our high vantage, we could make out the dome of smooth granite across the valley. It thrust upwards into the salmon sky, rounded and pale like a giant pearl. The world was growing more beautiful as I followed my dream of freedom. The faint glow of sunset melted the horizon into a golden line, Venus pretended to be the first star in the sky, a pinprick of silver-white amidst cooling sky. We watched in silence, as first one, then two, then uncountable stars burst through to transform the sky.

The heavens were reflected in the surface of the town below, lights twinkling along highways and suburban streets in symmetry with the constellations. Traffic, silent in the distance, streaked tail-lights and headlights through the stars below, playing meteor-showers and comets through the man-made ground-galaxies.

"Ever sung a harmony?" Beagle asked, in a hushed voice.

"Nope."

"Give it a try, I have the perfect song. You'll do the bass, which goes like this - " He began on middle C, and sang a simple melody. I hummed along like a bee, somewhere close to the notes he held. "Your words are simple : Starchild, born anew, free and wild, there's magic in you."

Beagle's own melody was more complex, and he sang in a resonant voice. Beagle wove such an intricate pattern above and below my notes that I was soon confused and my voice began to wander. I lost the path of the music and teetered off into the undergrowth of B flats and F sharps on the sides.

"Try to feel the music, as if it were a substance like clay," Beagle urged. "We are molding a harmony that has a shape to it. Try to feel that shape and make your voice follow it."

It worked better, and our voices blended until I could almost feel the fluid harmony pouring down the mountain slopes beneath us. I had never imagined that singing could be so uplifting. I was participating in its creation, no longer a spectator but a dancer, running notes through my partner's melody, dancing out into the night sky.

*Touch of the Heaven's so close tonight,*
*We feel the stars as they bathe us in light.*
*Maybe we could swim out from the Earth's rim,*
*We're living in a dream land.*

*How many times have we been here before?*
*This game of life doesn't seem to keep score.*
*Everywhere that we go, places that we know*
*Come to us from the old time.*

*Beneath all the plans that we create,*
*There is a pattern that governs our fate.*
*Beneath every new thing, a rhythm pulsing,*
*The heartbeat of the Universe.*

*We are each unique and new,*
*yet all the same, when we can sing true.*
*Sparks of creation, joined in elation,*
*We dance into Forever.*

# I AM UNLIMITED

The next day dawned bright and fresh. Sunlight spilled over the mountains and washed into the valley with the promise of good flying conditions. I decided to wait until there were enough thermals to sustain me. Once airborne, I was going to fly as far as possible northwards along the mountain chain.

Beagle set off on foot, eager to explore the peaks for hidden eagles. It struck me that he would be far more successful using a paraglider, but I bit my tongue, knowing that he had surely thought of that before. Besides, there was only one glider.

"Where will we meet tonight?" I asked Beagle as he left.

"I shall be where you are at dusk!" he shouted over his shoulder, and was gone.

A strange way of phrasing things, I thought. I was going to fly cross-country, I had no idea of where I was going to land that afternoon, or where the closest suitable campsite would be. Beagle had phrased his words as if he knew where I was going. Which was impossible. Maybe he had meant it metaphorically. I watched him vanish into the boulders to the north-east.

I sat for quite some time, in the sun. The boulders made me think of my beliefs, and how they had affected me in the past. I had lived for so long believing that I could not fly! And when I had moved that boulder from my path, the glory of what I had discovered filled my soul. I became a child again, in a world filled with learning and wonder.

What other boulders could I move aside? What more could I achieve with flying, if I was unlimited? And if I was really unlimited, why couldn't I fly over the impassable mountains at my back? Land on the tiny walkway across the dam I could see in the valley? Fly so high that I could see the curvature of the Earth? Fly without a glider? Vanish and reappear on the distant peak? Change my body into a bird? I started to doubt myself. If my mind had come up with so many limits, at least one of them must be true. If I tried to do the impossible, I could get hurt.

Then again, if I listened to such logic, I knew I'd not get far. I could see what was happening to my world. I was creating boulders to place in the path. I was limiting myself. I turned my logic on its head. Surely if my mind had come up with so many limits, one of them at least, had to be false.

Every day, every flight was an opportunity to try something new, to learn, to fly! I stood up.

"I am unlimited!" I said, out loud.

And I knew at once what I had to try that day. If I really was unlimited, it was time to master aerobatics. It was time for the loop.

I have spent many hours playing with my wing, testing its response to extreme rolls and pitches, diving it into deep spirals and whooping with the exhilaration of the pull-out. After each manoeuvre, the wing had felt a little bit closer to me, my mind and wing-body fused ever more. I had honed my recovery-techniques from extreme flight situations, so that when I needed to, I would survive the air's worst turbulence. I prided myself on flying smoothly and skillfully, ready to face any challenge with confidence. But there was one test of faith and skill that I had to pass before I could say that I had transcended my limitations of aerobatics. Just the thought of it made my blood go cold.

The loop is difficult to perform, on a paraglider. This is because the pilot is suspended underneath the wing on long lines. The pilot's weight keeps the lines taut and the wing flying. With a loop, you pass directly over the wing, and at this point, if I misjudged my momentum, I could experience weightlessness, whereupon I would fall into the canopy itself. The chances of surviving this would be slim.

The entry into the loop had to be judged to perfection, it would be a test of skill with dire consequences for failure. And there would be no practice, for a half-hearted tentative practice-run was exactly where the danger lay; with not enough speed, I would fall into the canopy. It was going to be all or nothing.

\* \* \*

There was a steady flow over my wing when I pulled it up, so I turned and ran out into the wonder of a new day's flying. The cliffs dropped away beneath my boots. The thermals were strong, and it wasn't long before I was high up, heading for the next mountain peak.

I became intent on coring the thermals, centreing on the rising currents and climbing as high as I could. A particularly strong thermal lifted me up so high I could see the desert plains behind the Cedarberg. I was well clear of the mountain peaks. My reserve parachute was safely stowed in the back of my harness, ready to save me from a loss of control.

Loop, chimed my inner voice. My stomach rolled over as the adrenalin flooded through me. This was going to be wild.

The sharp line of the horizon became a level in my mind, like the target-line in a gunsight. Below the taut wire of its clean divide, the earth, green and brown, a hard moulded crust of rocks and dirt and growing things. Above the wire, an infinity of blue. I was surrounded by invisible forces.

Up there no one can hear you scream.

My hand buried the right brake control to my waist. My wing slowed, wrenched back in the force of the braking, bending back in the wind. I could feel the judders of a stall gnawing at the edge of my wing, straining to engulf the whole, yearning to drag the lift off the aerofoil and consume the glider in its wild turbulence. I kept it at bay, working with my momentum and the brake control, easing up to let the wing dive, then turn again, dive then turn, buckling on the verge of destruction. The wing was banking hard and my momentum swung me far away from it on my lines. The G-forces increased, and I steeled myself for what was about to come.

Carving out the last of the turn, I began to fall under the canopy again, like a giant pendulum, Thor's hammer swinging through the heavens. Power surged through my body, into my arms. My heart spun like a crazy wheel in my chest. The wind screamed past my helmet, my lines vibrated beside it. I felt the gravity that collects at the bottom of a pendulum swing.

This was it, the checkpoint of my sanity. I snarled at my fear and laughed at it with the same expression, in the same instant.

As I felt the roll transferring across the wing to the left, as I began to climb out the far side of the pendulum, to rise into the sun, I buried the left brake control, watching the wing snap backwards on that side, all the energy transferred into the tight curl of wing. I wasn't properly over the wing yet. I needed more speed.

The target-wire of the horizon twisted in my vision, splitting the background in a vertical line that ran through the centre of my glider, through the centre of my body, through the centre of my mind. I rolled over hard to the right once again, committing myself to the deepest, hardest spiral I could envisage. Glider? Hell, no! This was a blade of fury, my challenge to the Gods. When I buried the right brake control, I would not let go. This one was going all the way.

My glider wound into the spiral as if scared by my aggression, frightened by the wild dizzying wrenching force that bound it to the centre of my own hurricane. I was flung out to the extreme end of my lines, they strained against my weight, holding me in the torture of my own making.

My vision narrowed. There was only a diminishing circle of colour before me. What had been on the periphery of my vision was gone. I clenched my stomach to force more blood into my head, to force some sight back. My right arm quivered with the exertion.

I leant my whole body over onto my left side.

As I approached the dreaded checkpoint at the bottom of the pendulum, I heaved a lungful of air. I knew that I was going to lose consciousness. It was too much, there was too much force pressing the blood out of my head, out of my heart, down into my feet. I had miscalculated the dive, there was too much momentum. I needn't have spiralled so damn hard. My life was crushed out of me.

I pulled down on the left brake control anyway, in defiance. Then I passed into the black borderland of unconsciousness.

Cold. Silence. Time and space collapsed into two dimensions, then with the smash of one last heartbeat, the world became one dimension only, a delicately savage dark point that contained everything that Is or Was or Ever Will Be.

I was at the end of the world. The singularity pulled at me, its black heart widened and I stared into a deathly void. A few coloured threads hung across the space like abandoned cobwebs. I clutched at them. Visions sparkled into my hands, moments of light that flashed through me, taking my attention away from the gaping void beyond the blackness. Each vision shot a new feeling into me, lit me with passion, filled me with purpose and intent to live, with yearning for the richness of being alive. With a thunderous roar, my heart beat one hammer-blow that shattered the illusion of Eternity and filled me with light.

A line divided my sight. One perfect, hard line with the deadly precision of a knife blade. It sliced my view in two, the Green of the above, the Blue of the below. Perfectly symmetrical expanses.

I fell, in a glorious, slow arc, living as gravity wrapped around my weightless body, breathing as the Earth drew me downwards.

As I swung past my glider, I yelled out in triumph.

# REMAINS OF THE DAY

After many hours in the air, I discovered a lake tucked away on top of the mountain, and guided my glider down to land on a smoothed col nearby. The air was turbulent close to the ground, but the winds were light, and I made a gentle landing. I was immediately immersed in the pungent scents of fynbos, a smell which had been absent in the sky.

I set up a small campsite on the western side of the lake, building a fire from dead wood. The faithful billycan was soon full of diced potatoes and bean-mix, and it bubbled away merrily.

The sun was just about to set when Beagle strolled into my campsite, swinging a dead rock-rabbit negligently by its hind legs, casual as you please.

"Supper!" he called out.

I was too surprised to greet him.

Not only had he found me, he'd brought a dead *dassie*. I was a vegetarian. To eat that small creature, to choose to end its existence just because we wanted to entertain our indulgent palates seemed so wrong. I was dismayed. I had never seen Beagle eat meat and had just assumed that he shared my principles. But there in his hands was a fresh kill. He was supposed to be such an enlightened being! I had looked up to him with his mastery of his reality and mystic skills. And yet, here he was, blood on his hands.

"I won't eat - that," I said flatly. I looked at him, judging him.

"What makes you vegetarians so holy?" he said belligerently.

"We have a choice, damn it! We don't need to kill to eat, we can live on vegetables and fruits. Give the animals a chance. They don't exist just to support your life, they have their own lives to live! " I was angry, he had shaken my expectations.

"But we have always eaten meat. It's natural."

"Natural? We've had many barbaric customs in the past, they weren't natural. We used to sacrifice humans to appease the Gods! We used to keep human slaves! We mass-produce animals to slaughter and eat. At some point you have to acknowledge what is happening is wrong!"

"And what if you're stuck in the wilderness, and you're there for five days without food, and your only possibility of survival rests upon you killing this dassie and eating it?"

"That's different. I would eat the dassie, but only if I had no other choice. That is survival. But you're not surviving, you can exercise choice. Have some of my beans."

"So if you're stuck in the desert, surviving, eating meat is good, but if you eat meat in the city, it is evil? Sounds mighty inconsistent to me."

"Just look at the system you are supporting!" The agony of a million wasted lives, cows grown for the slaughter-pens, no hope of completing their mysteriously peaceful lives, artificially stimulated and bred in vast numbers to satisfy the market, a market that chose to ignore the impact of its demand on the world. "Eating meat for pleasure makes you part of the murder."

I was hurt by his lack of perception.

"And those that consume meat somehow have no right to be enlightened, do not deserve wisdom and spiritual evolution?" He looked at me with a piercing glare

I looked away. "I didn't say that ..."

Good grief, I had always thought that, deep down, but never voiced it out loud. He had picked out a foundation-block of my towering vegetarianism. A block that, when held up to the light, was crumbling and rotten.

"Recognise the style of thought?" he asked.

"What? That I can judge who is worthy?"

"My way is the only true way and all other ways are evil."

A log popped in the fire. I looked back at him.

"Fanaticism?"

"Gotcha."

He was right. I was in need of a religious reconstruction. I didn't have the exclusive path to enlightenment. Come to think of it, I could not even be sure where my path led to. It just felt right. Vegetarianism was the only path that I could follow with heart. It felt right for me. That didn't make it right for everyone.

I tried to be open-minded. "So, thanks for the offer, but I choose not to eat meat. It makes me unhappy. What you choose to do is up to you."

Beagle smiled. "Yes! I knew you would get there. You don't become enlightened by having a lot of Good credits to your name and no Evil credits. Enlightenment is a perspective, not something you earn. Always remember that. And besides, eagles live on these things."

He lifted the dassie, and placed it on his open hand. Stroking it a few times, he set it down upon the ground. "Now run along!" he urged the little rodent, which suddenly roused itself from stasis and scurried away into the bushes. It had never been dead, just tired, dangling upside down in Beagle's hand.

My jaw hung open, and Beagle laughed until tears were rolling down his cheeks. "I thought we'd have a lively discussion with the dassie. I hadn't expected so much fun."

Beagle used the remains of the fire to heat up a can of spaghetti and meatballs. Meat, I noticed. Well, there went my religion. I collected more firewood, and stoked up the blaze with a few broken branches. The night gathered around the crackling flames.

"Why does the animal's death bother you so much?" he asked, in a friendly manner.

"Animals are such innocent creatures," I replied. "I guess I just can't bear the thought of slicing their necks and eating the flesh."

"Do you believe the animal has a spirit which continues to live in some form, or does it simply cease to exist when it is killed?"

"I think a spirit is indestructible, that it endures."

"So death is not the end of life, merely a transition from one state to another, or a liberation from one plane to the next? What if one can decide what creature's body you are going to inhabit during this incarnation, and had chosen to spend a short time in the life cycle of a cow. You, as the cow, were destined to be killed after two years, and this was understood from the start. Now you come along and say that the cow should be saved from this untimely death because eating meat is wrong, thus prolonging its life and the spirit within now has to go through the agony of being a cow for many more years than planned." His eyes twinkled.

"But you can't base your decisions on that assumption. There's no proof!" I objected.

"Neither is there proof that not eating the cow somehow improves the spiritual situation on this planet. You are basing your decisions just as much on assumption. You don't know the facts."

I contemplated this for a while, trying to make some sense of my beliefs. I could see his point.

"You said yourself that the Spirit is indestructible. How can you ever kill something then? The cow had a pretty good deal. Two years of great big fields, wonderful food, good company, no predators and a swift death. The spirit moves on, released."

"I don't know," I replied. "How can one ever gain the facts about death while you are alive? It is something you only learn about when you die. They don't pass out instruction manuals."

Beagle leant back into the darkness. "Don't be so sure. What have you experienced of death?"

I felt uncomfortable under his gaze all of a sudden. "There was a friend of mine who died in a flying competition. I always wondered where Doug's spirit went to, such an active guy, and all of a sudden he was no more. We continued with the competition the next day, in honour of his flying spirit. It was a strange feeling, flying in the shadow of his death, like he was still there, watching us from somewhere above. He changed flying for me. Before his death, flying was a big game. After that I had to really think about why I was flying, I had to find good reason to fly because it was about life and death. I still find inspiration and adventure, but it is more poignant, for I never forget. Doug spiralling into the mountain. The glider that didn't move again."

"Do you fear death yourself?" he asked.

"No, not really," I answered. Beagle raised an eyebrow. "The way I see it, everyone dies at some point. If my time is up, then I accept it, but I will always fight for life because I love living. I prefer not to think too much about death. It is unavoidable. So why worry about it?"

"That's just running away, hoping that you won't have to deal with death," he pointed out.

"But I'm going to die either way, whether I prepare for it or not."

"Ah, but there is a lot to be learned from death. Death gives meaning to life. The closer to death you are, the more alive you can be. Once you acknowledge that you have only a limited time to express who you are in this lifetime, what you do and how well you can achieve it become important."

I had to be honest. "Maybe I am afraid of death, deep down, but I just ignore it as much as possible. Why should I do otherwise?"

"Because you learn a lot by stepping beyond your fears."

I knew all about that concept. But death? How did you step beyond that, without being, well, dead?

"You can train yourself for death," said Beagle. "Every time you decide to change the way you are, you go through a small death experience. Death is letting go, stepping into the unknown. You can go a long way to understanding it by experiencing a conscious death."

"How does that work?" I asked.

"The conscious death? It's a meditation. You let go of your physical body. Let go of all the ties that bind you, and release your consciousness to the realm of pure spirit. You decide to change something about yourself, your habits, your attitudes, your behaviour. If you're really committed, you will experience a death of your old being and a birth of the new.

"With practice, you will come to understand the challenges of a physical death. If you are being forced to change and death catches you by surprise, it can be very traumatic. But if you are ready for it, death is a profoundly liberating experience."

I watched the fire burn down into coals. It, too, was dying, becoming ash. But it seemed to me that it wasn't liberated, it was just - gone.

There was a poem I remembered.

*Death separates us*
*For you died before I was born to this world*
*You stand in a realm*
*I cannot reach, recall*

*Turning around I face my own death*
*Your realm is beyond*
*yet in time I shall reach*
*That unfathomed space*
*Reach out, touch your face*

*If Time was to go*
*And I viewed life again*
*Would I not be beside you*
*My death would be Now*
*and my After, Before.*

# REAP OF THE HEART

It was a very dull day, the colours seemed muted. I had lost the awareness of energy and harmony. I felt listless. I packed up and made ready to walk to the launch site amongst the cliffs to the west.

"Same plan as yesterday?" I commented to Beagle, who was strapping on his backpack, flute in hand.

He gave me a strange glance, as if he was looking through me. "Sure, I'll be where you are tonight."

I chuckled. The ever mysterious Bartholomew Eaglefriend.

"See you later, then."

From the western cliff faces, flying conditions looked very similar to the day before. Light winds, slightly parallel to the mountain slope, weak morning thermals, no clouds - a government-regulation-issue summer's day, pale blue, cross country flying, for the use of.

The thermals continued to waft gently up the slope all morning, slowly gaining strength, but still too weak to sustain my paraglider and me. Visions of a long, hard hike back up the mountain flashed into my mind whenever my patience wavered. I sat in my harness, waiting to launch.

The sun beat down, drying the moisture from the bushes. The air was full of the incessant whine of cicadas. Sweat trickled down my spine. The breeze had calmed again, and the heat closed in. Drifting fluff from a dandelion floated in the air, a grasshopper zizzed by. Silence lurked under the bushes.

*pshheeee!* A small brown bird made a high-pitched call. It swooped down to catch insects, again, and again. Time ticked slowly by. There was another sound, from far away.

".. hh .. aaaa .." I scanned the cliffs and mountains to the north, trying to pinpoint the source of the distant cry. It was just on the edge of my range of hearing. I squinted my eyes against the sun, working over every surface I could see. Nothing. No people, no animals, no sign of disturbance.

Must be a dassie, or a bird, I thought to myself, scratching at the sweat running down my back. I was beginning to feel uncomfortable, waiting and waiting for the flying day to begin. The wind was still weak, but the heat was becoming unbearable, sitting as I was in one place. I needed to go and check out that call I had heard, something was still worrying me about it, I couldn't quite put my finger on it. I stood up, waited for the smallest of breezes and galloped off the slope.

I had to work hard to remain airborne, grovelling around near the base of the mountain in scrappy little pieces of lifting air. There were large patches of sinking air between the thermals. Back and forwards I flew, close to the rocks, sliding along the cliff-face, trying to eke out every single possible metre from each current before it dispersed and left me gliding down again. Finally, after nearly half an hour of scratching, I was carried aloft on the first good thermal of the day.

I glided along the mountain chain, gazing down, scanning the vegetation on the slopes for signs of life. I didn't really think I would find anything, so long after the call, whatever animal had made the noise was probably long gone, over the peaks and far away. Still, one never knew ... I turned into another thermal, swirling upwards again. Down on the slopes, something flashed for an instant, beside a crumpled, buckled shape. It was gone the next second, as I turned with my circling glider, away from the slope. But that one instant was all that I needed. My intuition did the rest. A silver flash. A flute.

Beagle!

"No!" I shouted at the sky, the dull blue of that ordinary day, impassively painted above my wing. "No No No!"

I banked my glider to face the mountain again, and raced towards where I had seen the flash. Something had happened to Beagle, I could sense it now, the sickening feeling as my stomach dropped away from me. Where was he? Further along the cliffs, comeonglider move. Flyflyflyfly you damned thing gogogo! I leant far forwards in my harness, searching for any clues to pinpoint Beagle.

I saw him a second later, his silver flute glinting in the sun, his crumpled body lying at the base of the cliffs, completely still. I couldn't fly my glider any faster, and I whimpered in frustration, wanting to be down on the ground, next to my fallen friend.

When I passed overhead, I could make out his pale face staring up at me. His body looked horribly twisted. His legs were bent back at an impossible angle. I shouted down, trying to raise some acknowledgement. He had to be alive. It was just not possible.

Beagle weakly raised one hand. Thank God he was alive! I banked over again, close to the cliff, setting up to land on the steep slope next to him. Rocks rushed by underneath me, the slope was treacherous and uneven. And the speed! I could not slow my glider down enough now, there was no wind to hold me back, and I was rushing over the ground, rocks bushes treesbushesslope! I was going to overshoot my landing spot, and beyond it loomed shattered rocks that thrust out of the slope like spears. I hurtled past Beagle, seeing his broken legs, the blood pushing up around his clutching hands, the pale grey of his face, the agony and pain in his eyes.

"My friend! I'm coming, I'm coming!" I banked out away from the slope, turning back to attempt a second pass. I was losing altitude rapidly, and with the speed I could find no safe landing area. Except for the fields, down below the mountain. Oh God, I was going to have to land down there, please let him be alive when I find him, don't let him die ...

A thermal enveloped me in lifting, hot air from the fields below, and I was lifted higher and higher, away from the landing, upwards into the sky.

"Not now!" I shouted at the untimely lift, and collapsed half of my glider to force a descent towards my landing site. What must have been a one-minute approach felt like an hour. I could feel sand slipping through an hourglass, Beagle's life slipping away; and me - powerless to aid.

My glider dumped me unceremoniously in the bushes, short of the field. I left it where it fell, unclipping my first aid bag from the harness and running. I threw my helmet off after another few metres, and sprinted up the slope. I had to get to Beagle, God, don't let him die, he's one of the good guys.

My heart felt like it was about to come out of my throat. I could not sustain the manic pace up the steep slope, I was going to kill myself in the process. Over the bush, over the rock, jump run jump. I slackened off slightly, but kept pushing. My mind was trying to pull my body up the slope, demanding that I didn't slow down, pushing me beyond the limit. I had to stop.

I forced myself to slow right. down. My breaths were coming in ragged gasps. I felt nauseous.

"Beagle - oh - Beagle my friend - I'm coming!"

I pushed up the slope again, forging a path through the thorny undergrowth, step by step getting closer.

"Beagle!" I shouted, tripping over a spiky bush, cursing.

"BEAGLE!" He had to be somewhere close by, somewhere in the area. I spun around, trying to identify landmarks. There was the tree I had avoided on my first landing pass, there were the spear-shaped rocks, he had to be further over to the north, just ahead of me. And then I saw his flute, raised straight up out of the bushes. It wobbled from side to side.

His clammy, white skin was covered in sweat. I looked at his injuries, aghast. Blood pulsed slowly out between his fingers, which he had clamped onto his left leg, well above the knee. What was left of the knee, at least. Under his hand was a mess - his black tunic had been torn into a wide bandage, wound tightly around his leg to slow the bleeding. But it was a hopeless attempt, the bone protruded through the sodden mass of fabric, his shattered leg bleeding through his fingers, soaking into the ground. His right leg seemed okay, but the way he was lying, his back had to be damaged. Oh Beagle, my friend.

I stripped off my shirt and tried to augment his leg-bandage with a new one, desperate to stop the bleeding.

"Try to press onto your pressure-point in that leg," I urged him. "Just there, on the inside of the leg."

"No .. strength," he murmured, "been .. pushing .. pressure .. point for hours."

"Hours?" I asked, alarmed, "You been here for *hours*?"

"Fell. just after. breakfast." He coughed, and my heart stopped. Blood splattered out of his mouth.

Jesus, this was bad, real bad. Massive internal bleeding, snapped fibula, huge blood loss, broken back. I looked down below his smashed leg, and saw the puddle of blood that had passed from his body. The ground tipped beneath my feet. He had lost litres of blood. Litres.

help!

I needed the professionals. Internal bleeding was beyond the scope of my first-aid training. I could splint the leg, and keep pushing on the wound, but he was bleeding inside. And then there was his back, I could not move him, I would paralyse him, if he wasn't already.

Looking out into the valley, I estimated the distance to the nearest farmhouse. A cold dread sank over me. There was a lot of slope, bushy terrain, and fields separating us from the world of telephones, helicopters and hospitals. A homestead was tucked away under some trees on the far side of a small cluster of farm sheds, four kilometres away.

I turned back to Beagle, and was met by his pain-wracked gaze. He looked even paler than before, and his lower lip trembled.

"I've got to go, Beagle! I can't help you, I need to call the helicopter. I'll run, I'm going to run as fast as I can, but it's going to be at least an hour before I return, another hour before they come to lift you out of here. Can you hold on, buddy, have you got the strength?" I squeezed his shoulder, leaning closer to make out his response.

"Sss-o .. cold .. doesn't hurt .. anymore. Mind .. only thing keeping .. alive. Don't want to die .. not now .. big mistake."

"You're going to make it! Don't talk that way, you're strong, you can survive!"

".. afraid of the end .. made mistake. Not ready."

"Just one hour, that's all you need!"

His chest convulsed in a heave that was either a laugh or a cough. Blood splattered out of his mouth again.

".. take .. flute .." His weakness showed so clearly now, the flute wavered in his grasp. I took it from him, placing my free hand on his other shoulder. His face was blank, but his eyes, oh his eyes.

".. learnplay .. understand .. yours now .."

"What are you saying, Beagle? I have to get the helicopter!"

".. you be .. eaglesfriend now .." He pressed something cold into my hand, closing my fingers with his, holding my fist in a weak clasp. His eyes searched mine through a haze of fear. I could see my friend trapped within the closing walls of his agony, fighting for escape, weakening every second.

Then his expression changed, for an instant. He looked up as if he saw an angel.

I heard the shriek of wind.

And then the bird attacked. In an explosion of feathers, an eagle struck Beagle's chest. Talons hit flesh, with a resounding impact that pushed Beagle further into the rocks. Powerful wings beat the air, hit my face. There was a high-pitched vibration that overwhelmed all other sounds. I could not breathe, I was too stunned. The eagle balanced and leapt into the air again, beating wings against my face, and dust in my eyes.

The silence was absolute.

I didn't need to look to know that Beagle's fight was over. My tears ran through the dust on my cheeks, falling onto his chest, dissolving into the blood, wetting his broken body with my grief. My friend was dead.

I cried freely under that dull blue sky, the sun could not warm my friend, and when my tears ran dry, my friend's hand grew cold in my grip, even though the sun shone in the sky, beating down on the brown rocks, the rocks that had shattered his body, his cold, cold body.

I could not cry anymore, because it hurt too much.

If I could not cry, I would work. I cleared out the rocks from a deep natural hollow that was perhaps fifty metres up the slope from where Beagle lay. The shock numbed my mind. I tried to scrape the grave deeper into the bedrock, carving out chunks with a slab of stone shaped like a shovel-head. Pieces of the tool kept snapping off in my hand, cutting my fingers until they, too, bled. Just like Beagle had, blood into the rocks, bleeding until he had died.

ohGodwhy .. why my friend, so strong .. why Beagle?

His body felt so light when I lifted and carried him to his final resting place, high on the slopes of the Saron Peak. A place that would look out over the setting sun, where the wind would blow with the strength of summer thermals, where eagles would soar. I gently laid his body in the base of the grave, propping his head up on some smaller rocks. Then I surrounded his body with fynbos, pulled from the earth to protect his body from the earth he would become. I layered the bushes until I could not see his body, until he was hidden from view. Then I began with the rocks, one by one, lifted and placed gently over his softened form. Small rocks at first, then bigger and bigger, then anything I could find, to fill that space that could never really be filled.

The gap in my heart that would be him, forever.

I worked through the day, the sun baking down on my naked back, sweat trickling into my eyes, stinging. I did not notice how thirsty I had become. All that mattered was to fill the hole. I carried rocks from further and further along the slope, piling them one on top of the other, building a cairn below the cliffs.

High clouds pulled in across the sky, softening the sun into a pearly-grey as the afternoon drew on towards evening. Shade by shade, the heavens shifted into a red sunset, with streaks of cirrus over the western horizon like talon scars. The fields were dappled in dark shadows. A bank of low cloud split the sky in a fine, second horizon, outlined in gold as the sun sank away from me, over the edge of the world, into the silent sea.

I found Beagle's flute, and raised it to my lips. All that issued forth from the flute was one plaintive note. The sun set, and it was dark.

# RAW

I slept in my glider, down amongst the rocks, below the grave of my friend. I drank some water, but ate nothing. I had no appetite, no desire to cook or clean or think.

A cold front approached during the night. In the morning, showers fell from tall grey cumulus clouds. I walked up to the peaks, and was soon wet. I slipped on the exposed rock. I sat out a heavy shower, watching the water drip off the shroud of my tented glider and puddle in the ground before me.

My world had shrunk to a circle of bushes. The sheets of rain drowned out all other sounds. I knew that out beyond the greyness, there were people and houses and cars and the city, busy in its daily existence, full of working people, striving people. So life goes on, I thought bitterly. I was the only one who cared about Beagle's death.

When the rain had ceased, I laid out my glider and ran off the peaks, out into the gathering wind. I flew because I did not know what else to do. The wet fabric created a sluggish wing.

"Help me to understand," I said out loud to the cold sky.

I wasn't really sure why I was flying, why I wanted to be up there, high above the peaks on a craft of fabric and string, so weak and flimsy. I looked down at the rough land, the shattered slabs of rock thrusting defiantly up towards me, the yawning gullies eroded by the harsh persistence of time.

I saw Beagle's body in my mind, broken at the base of the cliffs, and I saw mine, falling against the severity of the mountains. My bones felt weak, my body powerless, and I shivered in my harness as I rose under a cloud, building height for the crossing to the next ridge. I circled with wide turns under the greyness, gazing at the hard rocks and crags below. I fled from the threat of the cloud, which suddenly seemed too near, too full of treacherous lift and moisture.

The ridge ran directly north, so it deflected the westerly wind into a wave of lift, high above the plains. The wind was strong, and it grew stronger, threatening to push me back over the ridge towards the high peaks and the waiting rocks, those hungry rocks that lay glistening wetly from the rain. Sharp, hard rocks that hid beneath bushes, in tight gullies where the wind would be tortured into twists of turbulence.

Rocks, rocks, rocks the whole world below me was made of rock, disdainful of my fear, daring me to fall upon them, just once.

I guided my glider out into the valley, away from the ridge. I wished to be on the ground, away from the ominous clouds, the danger, away from the high winds of Fate, away, away ...

I landed not far from the little town of Porterville, a way out onto the plains. There was no place for me in the sky, amongst the shifting currents of elemental power, that place of infinite dreams and challenge. I was lost and broken-hearted, cold and lonely. I had lost the passion, the courage, the inspiration to fly. I had nowhere left to go. Nowhere but home.

Packing up my glider and stuffing it into its backpack, I could feel the depression settle like a dark cloak upon my shoulders, draining the last few colours from my aura, cutting the link between my mind and my glider, pulling me down.

I sat on the cover-flap of the pack, straining to close the zipper. It tore loose from the fabric. Damn it, it would have to stay that way. Porterville was half-an-hour away. I heaved my backpack up from the ground, alarmed at its weight. I could remember days when I had eagerly climbed mountains with this pack, but surely it could not have been this heavy?

High above me, against the white and grey of the towering clouds, in another world, a lone black eagle glided with outspread wings.

# ILLUSIONS

To protect myself from my mourning, I became insensitive, cold, and distant. I felt no pain, for I felt nothing at all. I was not alive, I was merely a body which moved about and performed its duties.

For months I worked in the city, but I cannot recall what I did or where it was. I can not tell that tale with any passion, for there was none. The depression pulled me below the depths of my soul to a cold and empty place.

With small certainties in every day, I slowly began to rebuild my reality, brick by brick. Every morning I would have a cup of coffee. Every morning the newspaper would come at seven-thirty. At midday

I would go to the shop and buy a can of cola. There was a television show every evening at five pm that I could watch. I could go to the movies every Friday night, and there would be something new on. I could add a few more bricks of habit around me, build a strong house to protect me from the emptiness outside. After some months of living in this way, I began to forget who I had been, before.

I believed I was healed.

The chatter of my mind kept me distracted and deceived.

It was amazing how many people drove to work alone, I thought, in their big Mercedes Benz's and BMW's, pulsing out exhaust fumes into the already overladen city air, sitting bumper to bumper in the traffic, impatiently regular in the morning ritual. If they would just team up, four in a car or even three, there would be no traffic jam.

Spent fuel created a wavering mirage above the cars.

What use was a three-litre engine in traffic that would move no faster than a bicycle, all the way to town? Why didn't they use something less polluting? I drove a small car, and it purred back at its sole passenger in the traffic, waiting for the queue to shift to the next lamppost, the next curve in the road, the next hill. Someone in the car ahead of me was gabbing away on his mobile telephone.

What could be so important that he needed to talk before he got to work, I wondered. Who really needed a cellphone? The monthly rental was so expensive. For a telephone? I had to be careful how I spent my money because there was never enough. But I really did use my cellphone, spending so much time in the traffic. I could call my friends so I didn't have to speak to them during work hours, which meant I had more time for work so I could be more focused and productive. Because I was contactable all the time I could get more work as a freelancer.

I was going to have to replace the tyres on the car soon, all four, that would cost a packet. I'd have to work for a while to pay that off. Look at all the unlucky sods in their cars, ties on, suits on, off to another boring day in the office.

I wasn't really part of the morning exodus to town, I was different. My job was challenging, and I could earn good money. Very good money. I was free to decide when to work. Although the shoot dates usually dictated the work-times, and there was so much work, I worked back-to-back, hopping from one shoot to the next. My agent had advised that it was better to keep working, so people remembered your face, so I couldn't really take a break. But I could if I wanted to, that was what was important, right? And the money was good.

I had bought a whole lot of new clothes. Not that I really had much time to use them outside of work, but they made me feel good. No more old faded blue jeans and the T-shirts from paragliding competitions. I had stylish trousers, and fancy shirts, leather belts, embroidered jackets.

A brunette was looking at me from a car over in the right-hand lane. I recognised her from the last shoot I had been on.

"Really cute," I muttered to myself. She winked at me, and I waved. "I would love to," I mouthed out the words, knowing that she would not be able to decipher them in the moving traffic.

Where did all these girls come from, and why all at the same time? Every time I became involved with someone, there would be others close by, testing my commitment. Then, when the relationship fell apart, all the girls would disappear again. My current girlfriend was Kim, just as cute as René.

Life was busy, and that was good. I had shunned the city before because I had just been unsuccessful, I had been earning a pittance when compared to the salary that I commanded now. And I was just an assistant - why, in a year or two I would be earning double, three times the money. Imagine the fun I could have, the things I could buy, the adventures I could afford to go on, the girls who'd be around!

I gazed out of my window at the rest of the traffic. No one else was watching me, they all stared straight ahead, intent on getting to work faster, gripped in the leviathan of cars, the metal twist-back writhing towards the city.

Oh well, so long as I was having a good time, that was all that mattered. Wasn't it?

And so the illusions wrapped themselves around me and created my reality. I got my enjoyment from my possessions, and before I grew bored of them I had to acquire more. Work was a competition, and I had to become better, work faster, work harder. Women were conquests, exciting confirmations of my own desirability. I saw the world through my ego, and everything revolved around ensuring my happiness.

Because I was so desperately unhappy.

I finally decided to take my paraglider out for a spin. Months had passed since I had last flown, and I could only remember that it had been fun, before the darkness. I hiked up the long path to Lion's Head after a rare early-wrap day, to catch a sunset flight.

Quite a challenge, really, launching from the radical steep slope of loose rocks. The wind looked fitful and treacherous. There were catspaws far out to sea, signs of an imminent weather change.

The deck outside the Club was full of the Bold and the Beautiful set - the young and wealthy folk socialising over sundowners. Kim was waiting for me, a cold beer in hand, so proud of her man.

She was surprised to see me walking in, with my bag on my back. She'd expected a stylish landing on the grass lawn, no doubt.

"Ah, the wind wasn't right," I muttered.

Her girl friends gathered around me. I was a lucky guy, there were four of them, all young and delicious. They all wanted to know about paragliding.

"Don't you get scared?" a willowy girl called Susanne asked.

"No!" I replied, a little too loudly. "It's safer than crossing the street, once you know how. As long as you don't try anything silly, and stick to the rules, it's like driving a car."

"But what if it folds up in the air?" Susanne asked breathlessly.

"Well, then I'd fall to the ground and die!" Her wide-eyed expression was adorable. To be honest, I had actually scared myself too. "I'm only joking!" I added quickly. "It's quite safe - the glider will re-inflate. It never falls all the way to the ground."

That was the truth, wasn't it?

As the sun set, a paraglider swooped down to a tiptoe landing on the grass, to a round of applause from the onlookers.

"Ahh, would you look at that?" I said. "The wind must have got better."

I told the girls a story about when I'd been flying at the coast and landed in someone's swimming pool, and they giggled in all the right places. The willowy one was looking cuter by the minute.

Kim pulled me aside.

"I am so glad you've got next week off, honey, I haven't really seen you for so long." She looked deeply into my eyes, running her fingernails gently up my arm. That always made a shiver run down my spine. *Brrr!* How I loved that.

"I have been over nearly every night," I reminded her.

"I know, I know, but I want to spend some quality time with you. To wake up in the morning with you and know that you don't have to rush off to another silly shoot or something. Just you and me, somewhere romantic, like Knysna. I've taken time off work until Tuesday, so we could have four days together." She watched my face.

"That is of course, if you want to." Her most persuasive look, that under-the-eyelashes-demure-please-make-me-happy look, my little nymph. I fell for it every time.

"Err .. sure .. sounds great!"

I had been thinking I should try to fly in the Cedarberg again, for a day or two, but that could wait. I hadn't really been in the air much, recently, and one needed to be on top of things to fly in the turbulence out there, otherwise it was a bit dangerous. I could fly later in the week, no sweat.

I remembered the last time I had been flying in the Cedarberg all too clearly. I had begun to go way off the rails at the end, before Beagle's death. Figured I was some kind of spiritual eagle being, started seeing all sorts of things in the air and on the ground. And Beagle! I had thought he was some kind of sorcerer, his command of the world was so impressive. In hindsight, I could see that he had merely been a dynamic personality, influential and coercive. But hey! one of the best; he had been my friend, and I missed him.

I twitched as the pain of his passing flickered through my mind. If only I had been there when he had first called ...

No! I wouldn't think of that. Last time I had been down that road, the depression had been too dark. He was gone, no changing the past. He had found his own end.

"What's wrong, honey?" Kim was all sweetness, melting around my pain, making me forget.

"No, nothing." I smiled at her, so cute and desirable. She knew nothing of my depression, or its reasons. I loved the way she took my mind off things, seducing me with her laugh and her smile. I was one really lucky guy.

"Another drink, everyone?" I offered. I enjoyed my new ability to pay for another round without feeling the barman dipping into my wallet. I was rich. That had to count for something.

\* \* \*

The winter drew the land into its stormy embrace, blowing the film industry back over the sea to warmer climes. I had more time to myself, shoots being few and far between, and I took to doing handywork in between, fixing a cupboard door here, a leaking roof there. Oddjobs. Odd jobs. Some of the work I enjoyed, others were certifiable disasters. Like the hole that I drilled in the kitchen wall to hang a painting - straight through the waterpipe. Handywork was never going to be my life's calling. I was merely paying the rent, doing time.

I had a few flights with my glider, cold, soaring flights in lonely places, never really getting too high above the ground, never flying too far. I mostly flew because my friends were out flying, and I was a paraglider pilot, and that is what we did. But winter came and went, and I logged very little flying time.

\* \* \*

"Marilyn is having a party tonight, should we go?" Kim had a towel wrapped around her freshly-showered body. She looked at me questioningly.

There she goes again, asking me for a decision for both of our lives. Dependency. Soon she would ask me if she was wearing the right clothes, what did I think, should she change? Why couldn't she have her own opinion, why did she need to use mine?

"Do I know Marilyn?" I asked, drawing Kim along. If she wanted me to make all the decisions, then I was going to tease her.

"Yes, of course you do! She was with us at the theatre the other night, when we went to see that Shakespeare thing."

"Hamlet?" I asked, stalling on the decision she wanted.

"Yes! She was the one with the blonde hair, with the big boyfriend - oh, come on, you must remember!"

"Yeah .. " I sounded uncertain, though I knew exactly who she meant. Sporty-looking girl, into sky-diving, a real party-animal. Boyfriend called Bruce, big guy, a bit of a rough diamond, ex-rugby player. They were a lively couple, and their party should be wild!

"What kind of party is it?" I strung Kim along, watching her.

"It's her birthday, so it's bound to be quite a bash. There's food and drink, we just have to go. Oh, and I bought her a present, so no need to worry. Are we going?"

"When does it start?" I side-stepped again, not giving her the decision she wanted, not yet.

"About eight, in about half an hour!"

"OK, let's go, sounds like fun." I savoured the moment, watching her face light up.

"Then into the shower with you!" she squealed, pushing me towards the bedroom and pulling off my clothes, one by one. I let her bully me all the way, resisting just enough to slow her down to a speed which I could dictate. By the time that we had reached the shower, I was naked and laughing. Kim's towel didn't last very long.

We were late for the party. The music was already cranked up, and we were drawn straight in to the dancing. Drinks flowed, people bumped into us, and the lights strobed across us all. The beat made me bounce, it made me jump.

*boomchitboomboomchit*

We met old friends and new friends. We smiled and danced together, we laughed. Bruce toasted Marilyn, and we all cheered. The music was good, someone turned it up louder. We moved to the rhythm. I kissed Kim in a dark corner. I looked over her shoulder and saw her friend watching me, a dangerous hunger in her eye. We danced in a threesome. We had more drinks. The night was alive with sound and sensation.

The music softened at last, and the euphoria of dance slowly dissolved. People began to bade the hosts farewell. A few of us joined Marilyn and Bruce on the balcony, overlooking the city lights, the curve of Table Bay under the night sky. Those with beer in hand had more to say, those who had shifted to coffee observed and tried to steer the conversation away from the brief forays into politics and rugby.

Bruce took a large swig out of the brandy bottle and leered in my direction. "I think all of these mystical religions are just a load of bull," he said. "I mean, folks go to yoga and meditation and this tai'foo'whatsit and the next thing they're 'spiritually enlightened'. Enlightened, my arse, they just get their wallets enlightened." He roared with laughter, and one of his inebriated friends slapped him on the back.

"Ever been to any meditation classes?" I asked.

"No way, you won't get me paying some rip-off artist to feed me some bullshit about the meaning of life, the universe and everything. I mean, if he was so enlightened, why would he waste his time trying to convince other people? Enlightened people should just float off!" He made a queer gesture, and his friends erupted into laughter again.

"So what's your answer to life, the universe, and everything?" I tried to put Bruce on the spot.

"Only the strong survive." He thrust his head closer to mine, enveloping me in brandy fumes. "If you're weak, you'll get flattened, or get your lights knocked out." He turned to his friends. "Hah, get it?

If you think you're enlightened, you'll get your lights knocked out!" His friends barked with laughter. Kim shot me a concerned glance.

"What if they are the only lights around in the darkness?" I asked, but the subtlety was lost on Bruce and his cronies.

"You seem to know a lot about this eastern mystic bullshit. You done any martial arts stuff, Bruce Lee?"

I could see where this was heading, I should have seen it earlier. I tried to redirect the flow. "I've done a bit of Karate over the years. What I really enjoy is meditation, it's calm and peaceful and very good for the mind. You should try it. You need it."

"Hey! I know judo, aikido, karate, jujitsu ... and many other Japanese words!" shouted one of Bruce's hulking rugby-player friends.

"So can you fight?" Bruce glared at me with bloodshot eyes. "Can you FIGHT!?"

"Brucey, no, he's our friend!" Marilyn cried out. This was probably a game she had seen played before.

"No, I don't want to fight, Bruce. I don't need to prove myself to you."

Bruce was appeased for only a second. "You'd prove yourself to someone better, a real fighter, but not to me, because I am not good enough! Is that what you're saying? I'm not good enough! I'll show you who's good enough ... come! Fight!" He kicked a plastic chair out of the way, and it went skittering across the balcony. He kicked my crossed legs off the railing. "Fight!"

"No Brucey no!" Marilyn was tugging at his arm, holding him back. He turned slightly, and raised a finger at her, his bloodshot glare full of violence.

"Marilyn!" he warned her, and she shrank away from him. That look of recognition on her face could only mean one thing.

This was fast becoming ugly. "Okay, okay, we'll fight," I agreed, "but there's a rule, otherwise I'm not playing." The option of not playing was unrealistic, I was in this whether I liked it or not. He had five rugby friends. I had none. The girls were not going to be able to stop this thing. I suppose I could have run away, but why should I be made a coward? "The first one to land a punch wins. This doesn't have to get bloody."

"Good idea. Go for it, Brucey!" shouted one of the rugby lads. The others nodded their heads and drank their beers. They were not so keen on a punch-up as Bruce was, but they would back him up if things got out of hand. I couldn't take them all on. If we had a real fight, I'd have to.

He stood glaring at me for a moment, then he pushed me roughly towards the stairs and the grass lawn.

"Okay, Mr Martial Arts, let's see you try to hit me before I flatten you!"

I'd done a bit more martial arts than I'd admitted.

I used the tai'chi technique of flowing with the opponent, softly absorbing and deflecting every attack, sinking and turning, yielding and shifting my body weight around a central pillar of balance. My training was all coming back to me in the heat of the moment.

Every punch that I ducked or blocked or deflected only served to fuel his drunken violence. I hadn't thought this through carefully enough. I had hoped that he would taken a few swings and lose interest, fall over drunk or something. He was being made to look like a fool, not able to hit a lightweight half his size. His friends jeered and hooted from the stairs. They were poised for action though. If I hit him now, it would lead to a full blown fight. He wouldn't take losing.

I realised what I had to do. Bruce needed to let off steam, otherwise he would become a violent animal. I was the only release-catch. If I took Bruce out now, hit his stupid drunken violent head with an easy blow, there'd be a free-for-all with one of me, five of his rugby pals, and most likely the girls getting hurt trying to pull us apart.

Let's get this over with, I thought, and stood still for just a second too long, giving Bruce his opening. His punch came whistling towards my jaw. At the last instant I ducked my head, and his fist smacked against the hard bone of my forehead. I let myself crumple back onto the grass, my head ringing with the blow, the cheers of Bruce's rugby corner drifting towards me through a haze of dizziness.

"Shit, he's got a hard head!" I heard Bruce cursing.

Not as thick as your brain, I thought. I hope you've broken a finger or three. I laid still, and groaned a little for effect.

Kim was on her knees in the grass beside me, teary-eyed.

"Are you alright?" she asked. People always ask you that when you patently aren't.

I raised my head slightly and winked at her. "Fine, we're going home," I whispered, then fell back on the grass, groaning again.

"You see, Kung Fu bullshit, the strongest survive!" Bruce roared. But he was holding his right hand in his left. I rolled onto unsteady feet and wandered off with Kim. I let her lead me to the gate. Marilyn rushed out to apologise. I waved her apologies aside.

"No harm done. We won't be back. Thanks for the party, it was good of you to invite us."

Marilyn looked forlorn as we backed up in the car and pulled off. Another social contact lost to her. I could have suggested an instant solution to her problems. She knew her boyfriend was an idiot.

Why was this violence coming to me, I wondered. What was I doing wrong?

# A HEAVY WORLD

I took a walk in the forest the next day, by myself. The sunlight fell softly through the pines, warming the bed of brown needles that covered the forest floor. Pines are alien to our South African mountains, but I still love the quiet and solitude that their plantations offer. The ground was springy underfoot. The lack of undergrowth offered unlimited paths among the towering trunks, unlimited freedom. The resin of the cones, the scent of the pine needles and the bark blended to enrich the air. I wandered for hours.

The world weighs heavy on my mind as I stride and stumble
midst crowded streets the hum of living encloses me in a vibration
and suddenly I lose my Vision, metamorphosed to a human Doing

I am                                not this
I was                             another
why                              am I here again?

                 all melancholy

I was in love
with the vivid patterns
intrigued by our connection            now filled with worry
                   can this be right?
                   am I really doing what I set out to do?
I can't see where I was          now I must go back
                   clinging to who I used to be

amid the sunlight against the tree
a distant memory of the other me
I feel the rush of care and reason
falling off my body as I lighten
with each breath air comes sparkling
into my new Being

I see far below and behind,
the place I was                    and yet it is in front as well
                                   and to the sides
One kaleidoscopic spark of manifested world - it matters not
I had visited there in the Now                    or Then


I lay down on the forest floor, sunlight streaming down through
the pines and soaking my body in warmth. The trees stood as tall
sentinels about me, appearing to converge in the sky above my head.
Somewhere high in the boughs, a squirrel scolded its mate as a pine-
cone came tumbling down from their perch. *Whizzzzzzzzzzthunk!* It
landed on the soft pine-needles and rolled harmlessly away, coming
to rest beside me.

Shallow. That's what my life had become. Completely shallow. I
picked up a pair of pine-needles, joined at their apex by a little knob
of resin. The drive in to work in the mornings. The daily chaos and
distraction of interaction with so many people, so many problems.
Day after day, the wheels turned, grinding on in the unstoppable,
persuasive rhythm of the city. I pulled at the pine-needles, and they
parted gently. At first it seemed challenging, enriching, a world to
build my strengths and my wealth. All too soon it had become drained
of its vibrant colours, the sugary delights and sensual distractions all
too plain, repetition after endless repetition. Oh, I had been here before,
a thousand times before. I kinked the pine-needle in half, then in quarters.

I thought of the party, the fight, forcing me to win or lose, to
compete, to be strong. In the long run, it left me with nothing. A waste
of time. It was a challenge of the wrong kind. What was my world
becoming, where was the magic, the passion, the fire? Why was I
back at the beginning, after so much growth, so many discoveries?

*Same reason you were here before.*

What's that?

*Can't say, that would be telling. The answer is the answer.*

The previous time I'd been so low, had been ... before. Before the
Big Sky Life, working in the city. There'd been that desire for security

that had kept me back, the fear of losing my stable life-style. That wasn't my problem now. I had no concern for security, I could stop my job the next day and be content. There had to be more to the issue.

A fear of missing-out-on-all-the-fun, fear of boredom? I crossed them off, one by one, pulling segments off the pine-needle in my hand, discarding the bits. What was it, that was preventing me from linking with my adventurous spirit of days gone by? Why didn't flying seem so important? Hell, nothing seemed important any more. I pulled another segment off the diminishing pine-needle. I was trapped in a box of reflective illusions.

*The world you see is a reflection of what you believe.*

So my inner world was also boxed in then. What was I hiding myself from? What fear had pushed me away from my dreams?

I knew then that I hadn't yet healed, I was still affected by Beagle's death. The fear had taken root in my soul.

I looked up at the trees, and considered things for a while. Climbing a tree would give me triumphant feeling when I reached the top. But once I looked around, I would discover taller trees, which stretched way up above the one I had chosen to climb. I would not be at the pinnacle of achievement. So I would climb down, branch by branch, and would lose the perspective of that lofty perch. Down and down, onto the ground.

Then I would lose my way, bumping into others who were, like me, lost on the ground. Only the memory of a higher place would keep me searching. At last I'd find the taller tree. Just imagine what I would see from the top. Why, I would be able to see the whole world! I would climb, and this time so much higher. I was surely reaching the pinnacle of existence. When I reached the top, I would find to my surprise that there were things called mountains, higher than me. And so a new journey would begin.

In the same way, I had broken through my insecurity, transcended the limitations of my walled-in world, and enjoyed the freedom beyond. But just because I had climbed the tree once, didn't mean that I would remain at the top. I had fallen out the tree. What was important was that I had learned how to climb.

After the tree, was a mountain. The challenges became larger. So here I was, boxed in by a larger fear than before - the fear of death.

It had taken me eight months to acknowledge the fear, and it was almost spring again.

I knew what I would have to do to master this fear.

# INTO THE BIG BLUE

It took me three weeks to work out my last contracts in the film industry, to cancel all future bookings, to explain patiently to my agent that, No, I was not going on holiday, I was quitting. No more, no more, I was out! Thank you, you have been a real sweetheart finding me all the work you did, I am sure you'll find another willing and able man to fill my place. I cancelled the television contract. Paid all the outstanding accounts. Adventures beckoned from the sky, making me eager to see the other side of Friday.

I screeched to a halt in an unwashed little white car in the car-park behind Lion's Head. I jumped out and strode through the dust, tore open the back door and heaved out my paragliding backpack.

I felt wonderful as I walked up Lion's Head, my body renewed as if some ancient, rusty armour had fallen from my limbs, leaving me light and free. I chased a butterfly that dared to flit across the path, and I had to catch my breath. Wonderful scents of the fynbos filled my nostrils.

Now I'm a bird, the bag's a wing.

I skipped along the path with my top-heavy backpack.

The laziness of the afternoon sun lay like sheets of gold across the idle sea. The air was warm, drifting inland towards the rising coastal peaks. How many times I had dreamed of this scene! The precision of the horizon splitting gold-flecked blue from the pale sky, the dark warmth of the rocks adding their encouragement to the buoyant air, the clean high feeling of being ready to fly. I ran with glider overhead, off and out into that wondrous space that filled all of my mind.

Gliding through the wind I felt cleansed, as if the stress of the days past had slipped quietly into the mountain, leaving me light and free. And it was good to swing out in a long lazy spiral, rushing air into my smiling face, the wing above me coming alive in the energy of motion.

High above the ground it is easy to feel special. Gliding slowly through the magic air of a summer's afternoon. What a way to live! I am flying.

Every second spent aloft I was living mankind's dream. Inventors had tried, through the centuries, to enter the majestic world of flight. Before that, dreamers had watched the birds. I was living the dream.

Below me, the sea soaked up the fading sunlight. The air became cool and thick as I approached the landing field. Smoothly gliding in to the centre mark, I flared long and slow, letting my feet slide through the green grass-tips and finally stop inches off the ground. Then in a whoosh the moment of anticipation became a soft landing.

It took me a few minutes to absorb the sight of the last seagulls wheeling above the field. They hovered over the golden sunset, playing with their gift. A beautiful moment.

As I wandered back from the field, another pilot passed me by, on his way home.

"Pretty boring flight, hey? There wasn't any lift. I only stayed up for five minutes."

I couldn't say a word. A fellow pilot, and yet his heart was in another world. I had been in that place, where that other pilot was.

"And yet, we flew," I said softly.

A chasm, narrow and yet so deep, separated my world from his.

# HOLDING THE VISION

*The time is ripe, oh grounded one,*
*to spread your arms out free.*
*For many moons and stars have turned,*
*in waiting for your lessons learned,*
*and oh how strongly has it burned?*
*that bird your mind can see.*

*The tide of Life flows in, draws back*
*within waters that noisome roar*
*some dreams that trailed on in your wake,*
*those visions kept for passion's sake,*
*and as the waves crash down and break*
*those dreams wash back to shore.*

*The sky calls out with space and might,*
*your wings spread wide and free.*
*That vision soon will leave your sight,*
*unless you hold on, oh so tight!*
*When clasped both hands, the dream of flight*
*Becomes your new reality.*

When I returned home, I was in trouble.

Kim wanted to know where I had been, why I was home so late.

"I promised Samantha we would join them for dinner tonight. How could you let me down? They were so disappointed, and I waited and waited. I was sure you'd come back on time, just like you promised you would. You promised! You never think of anyone but yourself!"

I stood in the hallway, my paraglider nudged against my legs, and we both felt guilty. My glider didn't say a word; neither did I.

"What is it with you lately?" she asked. "You've had this strange look about you all week, I don't know who you are when you look like that."

"Strange look?" I asked innocently, observing the way her eyes were naturally squint, the way her nose kinked gently to the side.

"You seem distant, you're on a high, but you don't share your thoughts." She looked at me scornfully. "Are you doing drugs?"

I laughed at her challenge. I wasn't even going to waste time arguing. Something had unsettled her, she was lashing out at me.

"What has happened in the last week?" she demanded.

"I've resigned from my job, I'm finished with the film industry."

"You've what? How are you going to pay your share of the rent? How will you eat? You can't just not work. What will you do with your life? You're not going to sponge off me, no way! I've had too many boyfriends that took advantage of me."

I watched her, trying to guess her real motives.

"And you've started paragliding again," she accused.

"I never stopped."

"You hadn't flown for ages, before, and I thought you had finally come to your senses."

"Come to my senses!" I flared. "What's wrong with paragliding?"

"It's a stupid thing to do with a perfectly good life. You're just going to kill yourself, jumping off mountains. What for?"

"You used to think that paragliding was exciting!" I objected. "You used to tell all your friends about your new boyfriend, the wild paragliding hero."

"I don't want you to be a hero. I want someone who is there when I need them, like I needed you tonight!"

I began to explain my passion for the sky, to try and make her understand where I went when I was flying, the beauty, the awe, the majesty. But I could see that she wasn't listening, she couldn't hear the meaning behind the words, would never understand.

She crossed the room and slipped her arms around me, a forlorn girl with a sugary-sweet voice.

"What happens if you have an accident? I know you don't have insurance. How are going to pay the hospital bills? And what if you get killed? What am I going to do? I'll be lost without you! I don't want to lose you, honey. I don't want you to paraglide."

In my heart I felt the stroke of a cold blade, ice cutting through warm flesh. It created a strangely alien pain, a shearing emotional hurt that was beyond physical agony. I almost cried out. Kim did not realise it, but what she had said heralded the end of our relationship. I held her in my arms and ran my fingers through her hair.

"Not even on weekends?" I asked in a choked voice.

Her face lit up, transformed from forlorn waif to joyful victor in an instant. Such manipulative mastery. I should have seen it before.

"Oh would you, sweetheart, would you stop just for me, to make me happy? Do you really love me that much?"

She kissed me seductively on the mouth, full and urgent with rich passion. Then she stepped back, and smiled broadly, as if the conclusion was foregone that I would leave behind my reckless ways. My comforting arms slid around her waist, my hands ran up her spine, caressing her body in reflex response to her sexuality.

She kissed me again, drawing me down onto the thick pile carpet of the lounge floor. But I was laughing quietly, inside.

You foolish, silly girl. You have no idea what you have done.

She had pushed just one step too far with her game of manipulation, and in so doing, had allowed me to see the act for what it was. I began to understand how I had absorbed fears and limitations from her over the past months. Without realising it, she had become more and more a part of my life, and with each passing day I had accepted more of how she saw the world, dissolving my own view to a combined perspective. I had wrapped myself in the security and comfort of her limited lifestyle. So much so that she felt she had the right to demand that I stop flying.

The coldness in my heart had spread, the cut became a gaping chasm that threatened to separate me from the warmth of her embrace, distancing me from the intensity of our lovemaking.

I did not join her in the climax - I was a world apart, drifting in my own galaxy of cold, quiet stars.

# MOONSTROKE

The moon was a brilliant disc of silver-white cut out of the cool velvet night. Thirty-seven stars were arranged in the random scattering of Creation, the remaining billion hid behind the moon and added to her brilliance. The landscape below fell away in black cliffs, silver rocks jutting out into space, sharp ridges clinging to the mountainside until they fell outwards in a tumble of foothills, spreading gently out into the dusty grey plains. The earth lay on its back gazing up at the sky in awe of the forces that had crushed it to this end. Every detail was drenched in silver, as if the source of this eerie light would claim the landscape as its own, transforming empty lakes to craters and leaving the plains blasted and pitted with meteorite-hollows. All sound sank away in that moment, yet an ominous thunder filled my mind. It felt as if the air became thinner and thinner, until it was almost of no substance at all.

I could reach up and touch the emptiness of Space.

The little town nestled in amongst the dramatic landscapes, with twinkling streetlights and front-lit clock-towers the dark squares that were houses with people and stoves cooking late dinners and televisions with comfortable couch pillows and little lapdogs scratching at the travelling itch - all of that, somehow, was below us, in another world. Civilisation did not belong up here. It was too beautiful on the mountain peak, too elemental. As we took in the immensity of the heavens above us, the town faded into insignificance.

There was just my pilot friend and I, two humans about to become part of a dark sky over a strange land, in a time separate from the years behind. There was only moonlight, air and the majestic form of sleeping mountains. The air churned in invisible currents as it explored the silver landscape. I had mounted a streamer, silver now, on a branch that stretched out far into space. Flying gently and straight in the wind the streamer told a deceptive tale. The air was far from smooth that night.

"Shall we go?" My whispered question shattered the silence. Neither of us spoke again.

Preparing to fly a paraglider at night left me with a strange feeling. Although every element of my glider was visible in the moonlight, they lacked clarity, yet had gained a weird property; a dreamlike intangibility that made me reach out and touch each separate part just to be sure they were real. By the time I was standing ready I could feel my entire glider, sensing its presence rather than seeing its form. When I walked to the edge of the slope I was wearing my wing.

The weirdness of the night demanded that I trust my own abilities completely - I had to believe that I could fly, meet the magic of the night with confidence.

We launched our spirits into the challenge of the night sky and our gliders and bodies followed. The wind swallowed the silence of our passage. We passed outwards, over dark rock, dark cliff, dark ravine. And then, with no warning, the air became a raging beast, buckling and twisting our majestic glide into a joust against an unseen foe.

My senses sharpened. Wild currents lofted me up high, then tipped me into troughs of curling treachery. The power bucked me viciously and relentlessly through confusing swirls of the dark unknown. Intuition guided me. I was flying on feeling alone, for my eyes only showed an ethereal landscape lit with lunar light.

Ahead of me, I saw my friend rising suddenly into the face of the moon, a black outline of the night leaping from the darkness into the only light. For a moment it seemed that the rest of the darkness would be drawn with him across the light to swallow it completely, plunging me into blackness. But then the night reclaimed my friend as he plummeted in a down-draught. Seconds later, I was where he had been, falling from the face of the moon and into the night.

As suddenly as it had begun, the turbulence vanished. We were propelled out from the mountains into the valley. The transformation was breathtaking; the air was smooth, the wind calm, my glider was a curve of beautiful silver-white overhead, intriguing patterns crossed her surface where the seams in the fabric changed the moonlight to moondark. I breathed in deep draughts of relief.

Clean, clear, invisible air filled my mind. I looked up once again, and realised with fascination that I did not have any lines connecting my glider to my body. Nothing was visible against the brilliance of my wing and the deepness of the night beyond. Yet she responded perfectly with just the thought of a turn, the gentle touch of my hand on the control line and my glider high above in the sky eased into the new direction. I loved my glider for that.

We were immersed in unbroken silence. The silence stretched out to the far horizons and seemed to bind the visible world into a tighter fabric, for there were no sounds to fill out the gaps. I flew, moonstruck, over a world that was simple and new and strange, and I wanted to be in that vast, quiet world forever.

And yet there was a sound, a gentle musical sussuration as if water droplets were chasing each other over a tight drumskin. My glider cut smoothly out through the starlight, as silent as the landscape below. My gaze dropped to my body, which was levitating with infinite ease over the tumbling foothills. I was bathed in moonlight, but where was the sound coming from? It was impossible to make out the details of anything in the light.

Although everything was clear, there was some dimension that was warped, mutable as in a dream. The light of the moon fell upon my body and as it touched me the light burst in puffs of silver dust. There the light became sound and tinkled softly over me as it was drawn away in the gentle rush of passing air.

I carved through the night thick with magic.

I looked out toward the landing field, dark uncertainty on the edge of the little town. The sound of the moonlight faded and was gone. Soon the smell of grass was floating up to meet me and I banked a final turn, swinging my feet out to absorb the impact that would define the final moment of my flight.

But where my feet should have contacted the earth with a solid thump! there was nothing. Something was wrong. I pushed my feet further down, through the dark surface of the grass and deep into the soil beneath. The grass seemed to shimmer and shift in the darkness, as if unsettled. Then the world began to swirl around me and I could make out the reflection of the stars in the grass.

Stars! I must be landing in a lake, I thought as the wind rippled the surface of reality again. I was struggling to hold onto my grasp of who I was and what I was seeing. I could not feel my harness anymore, I felt light and soft, lying rather than standing and yet I could see the stars in the lake with perfect clarity. I reached out my hand just to be sure and could see its blackness against the pinpoints of light.

The surface of reality rippled again, huge chunks of the sky were blocked by a blackness that buckled and twisted across the lake. I put my hand down to steady myself and contacted something solid. I clung onto the object.

Relief washed over me, and my confusion faded. I felt wood in my hand. I could feel its texture and its smooth, clean corners. I ignored the fact that the sky was being battered apart by what looked like a massive flapping curtain. The wood was certainty, the wood was solid and as long as I could hold onto it I would have a reference point in this strange world. I would be okay. I ran my hand over the wooden object that was looking more and more like a table in the dim light. The curtain of dark flapped gently in the night breeze that swirled in through an opening. An opening that was looking more and more like my bedroom door.

I rose from the softly piled blankets of my bed and padded across my carpet to the curtain and the breeze. Stepping outside I was bathed in quiet radiance. The moon was a brilliant disc of silver-white cut out of the cool velvet night. Thirty-seven stars were arranged in the random scattering of Creation, the remaining billion hid behind the moon and added to her brilliance.

Beneath the sheets, I could make out Kim's sleeping form. Her hand was stretched out in a subconscious display of dependency. Come back, it said, I need you with me, I want you beside me in my world.

"Sorry, sweetheart," I wrote, "but I can't come back. I have stepped out into the magic of the night. I must leave you now, alone. Goodbye, and thanks for our time together."

I propped the note up against the flowerpot on the bedside table, sure that she would find it in the morning. Some would call it cowardice, to run away from a situation that has become un-nourishing. I didn't care, my passion to follow the dream was powerful and all-consuming. It was simply time to go, I had lived through my dark night of the soul. I packed a travel-bag full of clothes, raided the pantry for a few essential supplies, hoisted my paraglider into the car, and was gone. The last and sweetest seduction of my city-life slipped away, purring in contented sleep amongst the rumpled sheets of a soft bed in a safe room below the thick roof of a tidy house in a quiet, suburban street.

The moon had set. Above the car, there were stars everywhere.

# IN THEIR TALONS

Dawn surprised me with a view of the Dasklip Pass. I rolled my head from side to side, trying to ease the stiffness out of it. Sleeping curled up in the back seat of the car had seemed like a good idea at the time. It still made no sense at all, how I came to be there.

I opened the door and stumbled out onto the gravel road. I looked out at the waking valley, the greens, browns and golds of the fields coming to life at the sun's touch. Smiling, I stretched my arms up as high as they would go, remembering. The moonlight. The stars. The tangible magic, bursting off my body.

I wolfed down a breakfast of bread and sweetcorn, then sat on the steel hang-glider ramp, surveying the weather conditions. A time like that would have been when Beagle would have played on his flute, honouring the morning.

Good old Beagle. I still had his flute - it had been stashed away in a sock all winter, waiting for me to play it. I had tossed it into the car when I had packed last night. Things were beginning to work with that strange harmony again, the rhythm of the Big Sky Life.

When I opened the sock and shook the flute out of its bag, something else tumbled out and fell through the gaps in the metal grid of the ramp. I heard the object drop into the bushes below. I scuttled in underneath the ramp to find it.

My hand touched something cold and hard within the leaves, a small thing, complex in its convoluted shape. I pulled it out and drew a sharp breath. It was Beagle's pendant.

I had forgotten all about it. As I turned it over in my hands, I began to recognise the design in its tangled black and white forms. The shapes were the talons of two eagles, one black, one white. The talons were locked in a battle for supremacy, but seemed perfectly matched, being both the same size and shape.

The pendant was intricate and finely carved from some hard polished substance, seeming as cold as stone, but as light as wood. I couldn't identify the material, it seemed uncannily smooth. Threaded through the apex of the pendant was a thick cord with a sturdy clasp. I held the talons up, poring over the intricate curves and designs. Beagle would have wanted me to wear this. I vaguely remembered him saying something about it when he handed it to me, before he died. Funny how it only reappeared in my reality when I had escaped from the city to the Big Sky Life once again.

I drew the cord around my neck, and closed the clasp. Clambering out from under the ramp, I emerged to the sunshine and still morning air. It would be a while before it became flyable. I had a few hours to think, to explore, to discover myself again.

The flute issued forth silver notes into the still, morning air, some melodious and melancholy, others wavering and diverging under the unpractised guidance. Each note vibrated with a clear resonance that stimulated memories within me. The air began to fill with phantasms and images of my past.

As I saw each image and acknowledged myself in that world, I became connected to the times gone by. I felt myself acquiring a perspective I had so enjoyed, so loved, as I watched the energy pulse out of the ground around me. The vibrant life in the trees! The subtle flow of the companionship between the plants!

I saw two black eagles (had they been there before? - they appeared as if out of thin air!) acting out their glorious courtship, the male performing aerobatics with masterful precision. Ah, the sight! How blind I had been! Only now did I understand, when the sight returned, that it had gone before. There was a living, undeniable power all about me. I called out a mental 'Hello' to the beautiful pair, just for fun, to see if I could still do it.

[Hail! young eaglefriend] came the joined mental reply, two thoughts in perfect harmony. I was stunned.

Eaglefriend! That was Beagle's title, not mine. Wasn't I supposed to be Skywalker? What did they see in me that was new, what had changed? Why should I be likened to Beagle at all? I was a pilot, he had been a mystic. My intent was to perfect flying, his to perfect communion with the eagles.

I looked down at the pendant, dangling on its cord. The two eagle's talons, locked in combat. The eagles had called me Eaglefriend, with a crisp telepathy I'd never experienced before.

I suspected that I was taking more of a step than I had anticipated, something beyond flying, something beyond mastering my fear of death. The eagles had passed, gliding away to the south, leaving me to fly, to follow when my time was right.

\* \* \*

The wind blew too strongly all day. Nightfall found me camping in a pine forest. I knew that the eagle's nest was amongst the cliffs nearby. It was a wild, abandoned and magical place.

I curled up in the folds of my paraglider, pulling my jersey up over my head to protect me from the crawling night insects. Sleep claimed me swiftly. I dreamt of two eagles - one pure white, the other as black as space. They clashed in a fury of might and magic, falling from the sky with talons locked, the sky behind them exploding in a chaos of thunder and lightning. I felt the wind rushing by in a howl, the world spinning in the final acceleration of their impending doom. Down and down they spiralled, their cries defiant. I cringed as the inevitable moment of impact loomed. The ground rushed up, warping outwards from a still point in the centre, with horrendous speed ...

My body jolted in a pulse of mental anguish. I awoke just before the instant of enlightenment and annihilation. I fingered the cold pendant that hung around my neck. The black and white talons, tangled with each other.

# SYMPHONY OF MIRACLES

The wind ripped at my clothing and blew my thoughts of flying away, out into the valley to be tumbled in the rotor and be blasted to fragments. It was a dry, hot wind that had snarled and gnawed at my glider late in the night, tearing through the pine trees, bringing tales of the huge mountains that had twisted its passage, smashing it against the rockfaces, torturing its purpose, till the wind had emerged like an angry beast. Its fury resounded in my ears.

No birds flew. My glider and I huddled midst the rocks, and I wrote poetry. For hours I played with bundles of magical words of rhythm. The day was a write-off, completely unflyable. And then a little miracle happened.

Something shifted in the ether. The sound of gentle breeze touching a pine tree. My wind-streamer stuttered out the passing of a thermal. A defiant call of the black eagle pierced the soft moment. I looked up, and there was the local pair of pilots turning their feathered gliders gently; lazy circles in an azure sky. The wind had vanished; the beast had blown out into the valley and we were left with a miracle of quiet.

My glider lay poised behind me on the slope, waiting for my command to lift and fly.

I checked my carabiners to see that they were closed. They felt like a part of me, I mused, and yet they weren't really 'me'. The boundary of the real me was inside the harness. If someone touched my shoulder I would say that they had touched me. But what of when I undressed at night? With the flying suit removed, did that *me* become smaller, just my naked body? And what of the food I had eaten, only moments before? Although inside my body, it was not really *me*, was it? When did it stop being a piece of bread and start being *me*? It was only fuel for the systems in my body. Those systems were not *me* either.

I know what my body looks like, and therefore I know who I am. But was that the real truth of it? If I had lost my legs in an accident and scarred my face terribly, my body would be very different. Would I be any different though, essentially, deep down? Psychological changes aside, deep down the real *me* would still be the real *me*. I was still the same person with the same name. I was the same being on the continuum of my life. My body belonged to me, but it was merely a vehicle.

A gust of wind tossed my glider up the slope, and I ran with it to control its restless shape. It was time to fly, for the wind had strengthened at last. I pulled my glider up until she was a weightless curve overhead, tilting and twitching in the air.

I stand naked before the sky, I realised, for all that I am, is spirit.

I stepped out into an unlimited adventure.

The memory of the strong wind lingered in the grass, in the tired branches of the trees, in my thoughts around me. I searched the ground below rapidly; crystal clear dams, the dust from a toiling tractor rising in a lazy vertical column, gently turning in the still air. I eased back into my harness, the knots in my stomach relaxing as my glider soared into the first thermal and I banked her, circling to join the rising air.

I tuned my two-way radio to the paragliding channel, and it crackled to life. "Hello, Hello. This is Jan." A paraglider pilot! I had thought that I was alone in that huge sky. I grinned; Jan Voster was an old friend. What better person to share this day of miracles with a man who had been drawn back to the sky after recovering from a bone-shattering accident. Of all the people I could think of, Jan deserved this day more than anyone.

"Hi, buddy! Where are you?"

"Teenage Tit, five hundred up." It's a mountain peak that, well, looks like it. If you've been in the mountains a bit too long.

"You better start racing, because I'm right behind you." Nothing like optimism to get you high. No need to disclose the fact that I was over ten kilometres behind him and that I was sniffing amongst the bushes half-way down the mountain slope, desperately looking for lift.

I still hadn't caught him by the time I'd reached Bumpy Peak, a legendary mountain of many moods. Whereas Jan had risen out of the valley here to kiss the sky at two-thousand metres above sea level, I was wrapped in turbulent sinking air. *Whack!* My wing collapsed on the right. I headed away from the mountain. *Thump!* My wing tilted dangerously away from me.

"You'll have to do better than that if you want me to repent!" I shouted in defiance to the turbulence, and regretted my challenge at once. I shuddered through a messy area of aerial speed-bumps. My stomach didn't enjoy the badly constructed detour.

"You have the wrong guy, I'm a little angel," I pleaded with the Sink Monster, but no one answered me back. Silence.

Hushed air is worse than bumpy air sometimes. You don't know where the turbulence will come from next, but you can feel its presence waiting, lurking, stalking.

"Okay, okay! I repent!" I left Bumpy Peak to its temperamental humour and scuttled off along the mountain chain.

I glided for some time, softly sinking below the peaks, watching with resignation as more and more ground filled my view. An early landing at this remote part of the flight would be disappointing. I looked down at the fields and imagined myself walking out to the road in the heat; it was quite some distance. My fate almost sealed, I sank faster toward the fields I was dreading.

Not a moment too soon, I jolted myself out of the reverie. I was creating the sink with the way I was thinking! I was focusing on the landing, there in no-man's-land, and my senses were simply following my mind's command of staying in the sink.

*Believe. Expect a miracle.*

Up, up! I thought, believing myself climbing high above the valley floor. I could feel the crispness of the altitude, I could smell the sharp whistle of the air rushing over my glider, I could see the earth falling away under the spell of gravity. Flying out into the valley, low over the foothills, I released the vision and allowed my mind to find the solution.

A vague image of a thermal began to form. I tried to coax my vision out from the shadowy recesses of my mind, but it dissolved in the bright sunlight, leaving me staring out into the clear summer air. I closed my eyes to limit the illusion they were presenting.

The vague image of the thermal returned, billowing upwards off the plains to my left. I turned towards it and felt the image strengthen as I gave my perception encouragement. Opening my eyes, I saw nothing new. But I could feel the thermal building and rising in the internal picture inside my mind and I made small adjustments in my heading to meet the thermal head-on.

With a rush of excitement, I rode my glider upwards, banking and twisting until I found the core of the lift that would take me up into that cold, high place where there is just sky. The ground sank away under the spell of gravity.

From high, I soaked up the awesome view. Fields, neatly ploughed and fenced by years of toil, all part of a giant tapestry of greens and browns, the boundaries reclaimed by the vastness of the Earth. I was immersed in the view; it was all around me below me on the sides and above, so much richness and space that I could never hope to absorb it all. The horizon was woven into a white haze that hid the edge of the world - for all I could see, the sky and the earth ran off to infinity in all directions.

I had almost unlimited choice before me. Each direction I chose to fly in would be a different flight, a unique adventure, with different challenges, different lessons, different landings. From this place I could surely glide forever.

Forever turned out to be about ten kilometres, thanks to the ever-present sink.

"Is that pilot below me planning to land?" came the witty greeting on my radio. Jan was way above me. I supposed that from where he was, I looked to be very close to the ground. Wisecrack!

But then looking down, I noticed that from where I was, I looked to be very close to the ground too. I had to work anything and everything I could find that was going up.

Some warm air ran out from the sheep-pen, past the farmer's children in the little blue portable pool on the small green lawn. The warm air milled about in the farmyard for a while, threatening to leave me to a dusty fate while it chatted to the chickens and the dog. Then a puff ventured onto the barn roof and it was up and away, drawing the surprised bark of the dog and some hay along for the ride. My wing bumped up for a quarter of a turn and I held on for all I was worth. Gradually we sneaked away from the ground again. I was a bird reborn, offered the gift of flight once more.

"Where to from here?" Jan asked, slowing down next to me.

"Let's build up height to clear the Constriction then run straight down the valley," I anwered.

The Constriction gaped below us, where the river cut a narrow channel between close-set foothills. It was a stretch of tricky flying. Not the kind of place where you want to be low down, looking for a landing field. But then I don't think that was what Jan had intended.

There, on that beautiful sunny afternoon, high above the plains of Citrusdal, wind in his hair and with a smile, Jan Voster flew into the Sink Monster. And he sank like a stone, down toward the Constriction. The Sink Monster took all of his altitude, it robbed him of his pride, mocked his skill and seemed intent to leave him as a creepy crawly thing that must scuttle about on the Earth.

I held my breath as Jan sank down into the turbulent air of the river gorge and desperately searched for a landing space. At last he landed on the steep slope next to the gravel road. I breathed a sigh of relief. He was okay.

And I was alone again. A sheet of midnight blue lay below me, streaks of sunlight glistening off its wet, perfect surface. In parts of the dam I could see the colour of the sky, in other parts it was a mysterious obsidian. Not a breath of wind rippled the water.

When I approached Clanwilliam town, I was barely above the gravel road, following a car that would hopefully trigger a thermal. When it came, it carried me in the climax of the day, softly, gently over town, in a thermal poured from mellow sunshine.

The cows were at peace in the fields, the people lazed on the banks of the dam. I sneaked by, a butterfly against the cooling sky.

All the stored warmth of the valley rose then to carry me. I flew far out past the town, without turning, without needing to, just gliding on the magic air.

As I landed, Jan arrived in his car. He and his driver had followed me from the Constriction just to see that I had a safe landing. And did I want a ride back to Porterville?

As I walked up the mountain pass that evening I could hear the faint chirping of the crickets above the crunch of gravel underfoot. The stars became pure white in infinite darkness. The gentle whisper of the warm night breeze played across my ears, and the memory of my day filled me. As each memory took form I heard music, it swelled out of the ground, through the rocks and the trees. The air was thick with it.

I saw my flight as a melody supported by an orchestra. I had flown, like a soloist, through a Symphony of Miracles.

# LISTEN TO THE SKY

The next morning, sitting all alone up on a high rock, overlooking the valley, I tried to contact the eagle pair. I had almost given up trying when I heard a defiant cry, more inside my mind than outside. I looked up towards the sun, already mid-way across the morning sky, and saw them. Two tiny black specks against the vast blue canopy, their turns barely distinguishable next to the sun's glare, wingtip to wingtip, wonderful masters in their aerial kingdom.

My friends, my eagles, I can sense you so clearly! How did you get up there, so high? Where are you going to? What is your real purpose? How many years have you been here? Where is Sundancer, that special eagle of the Beyond? Can you hear me?

The eagles parted in a wild flurry of flapping.

[Never do that. (pain). Study silence.]

Too late I realised what I had done. I had bombarded them with raw, disorganised thought. I wondered if the pendant I wore was some kind of an amplifier.

"Sorry. How did you get so high?" I strained to keep out the other thoughts, a whole host of them that mobbed the door to my mind, banging on the frame, demanding to be let in.

Jeez, that's not important! I thought. I had an opportunity to ask eagles about telepathy, about spiritual matters, anything. Who cares how they got so high? They fly there! Then again, conversation was important, I couldn't just rush in and start on deep questions. But

Beagle used to do just that, he always had. And I did really want to know how to fly as they flew.

The eagles were stumbling in the sky.

"Oh damn, I'm sorry," I projected, clamping down on my mental dialogue.

[study silence] came the chiselled reply.

They turned and glided fast, in unison once more.

New thoughts assaulted me, but I ignored them, I kept my silence. I hoped desperately that I could be still until the eagles were out of range, protected from my barrage. But it was difficult to let them go, those eagles who held the key to so much of what I wanted to learn, the wisdom of years in the sky.

"Don't leave me!" I cried out.

[We return with the silence.]

Then they were gone; the sky was clear.

Thoughts tumbled down around me, released from the moment of forced silence. Important thoughts, arbitrary thoughts, thoughts about the eagles, about flying, images of clouds and wings and aerial ballet. The mental river cascaded over me, purging questions and dialogues and self-doubt and fear and worry and imagination and visualisation. Finally my inner voice, previously hidden beneath the babel, slowly surfaced.

*Observe your thoughts. That is the secret.*

There were gaps between the thoughts that raced across my mind, periods of blankness. I tried to hold onto them, to extend them.

*Your thoughts are as a pool of water, currents swirling, wind blowing, ripples disturbing the surface. You will never succeed if you project your thoughts from within the pool, for every thought creates its own ripples.*

A smooth pool of water. A quiet, still pool with no ripples.

Quiet. Still.

*Be an observer in your mind. Be above the pool, observing.*

A single disturbance in the pool as I lifted out from it. Concentric ripples radiated outwards.

*Find the single thought you want to look at. Be passive. Observe.*

In this mental state, I had a view from above. My current thoughts, there, below me, a thought of flying over a desert formed in the pool. Next to it there was a bird of prey, diving to the kill. On the far side an image of a wave, breaking. They swirled like patterns of oil on the surface of the mental pool. I tried to hold up the thought of the wave, bring it out for observation.

I soon found that thoughts were more slippery than wet fish. After some time I couldn't keep my head about me any more. I played Beagle's flute instead.

I watched the notes of the flute float over the pool of my mind, calming the water. I found I could just watch the melody and get lost in the twists and turns of each new piece. There were pathways that followed the rhythms, subtle shifts from certain notes to others that somehow just felt right. I floated along for hours, thinking nothing in particular, all the time learning to calm my mind. It was ironic that I could find the silence in music.

At last I looked around me. The sun was high overhead, veiled in pearly-white clouds, and the sunlight filtered down diffused and milky. The shadows were softened beneath the rocks and trees. There was a strange atmosphere, as if something musical had lingered in the air even after I had ceased to play on the flute.

It was almost windless, and far in the distant mountains I could see the dark smoke curling upwards from an invisible fire. The day had an ancient, timeless feel about it. I scanned the sky, half-expecting a bronze-scaled dragon to come flapping by, breathing fire before retreating to its lair in the distant peaks. I could see which peak it would retreat to; a tall, pyramid-shaped massif that loomed from across the valley. The peak was suddenly illuminated by shafts of sunlight that penetrated through gaps in the clouds, making it stand out proudly. It intrigued me. In a flash I was there, climbing the jagged rockfaces that fell down to the rivercourse below.

Thus I found myself hiking late that afternoon, my backpack filled with a light collection of food, water and warm clothing. I'd left my paraglider behind - it was too big a peak for a heavy-packed ascent. But I'd been called to climb, and climb I would.

The sun sank in the afternoon sky, and hints of colour washed into the high white clouds. The clouds had thickened during the day, probably an approaching cold front. There was little threat, I thought. At worst a light sprinkling of rain.

I reached a thriving rivercourse. Ferns and fine-leafed trees crowded in against the river. Each tree created its own space, even when twisted around another.

I took my boots off and waded into the cold river, delighting at the sensation. I dug my toes into a patch of river-sand, smiling blissfully. A puff of disturbed silica drifted downstream in the current. The water upstream was crystal clear, fresh from its source.

Two butterflies flitted along the riverbank, swirling up to the green tree-tops, then gliding down to the water once again. They had colourful wings of orange, yellow and black. They took it in turns to lead, playing bare centimetres above the water, flying low and fast, pulling up and away, then swooping down again. I envied them their grace and freedom, wonderfully adept, true flying forms.

Flit, flit, glide .. flit, flit, tumbleglide .. circle, flit, glide.

Did they have enough mind to be playing this as a game, or were they merely jerking about in random motion? They just seemed to be having fun.

The butterflies ventured off further upstream, investigating a dark pool. I could just make out their colours through the overhanging branches of the trees. I tried to project my mind to where they were, to follow them and watch them, the way Beagle had shown me to.

At first I only drew a vague image of colour and light, which competed with the river-scene. I closed my eyes, and tried to still my thoughts, following the movement that I could see within.

Slowly, my vision began to clear, and I could make out the water (greatly magnified) rushing past underneath me. I was chasing (my partner) a butterfly of brilliant orange, (playing) flying as fast as my wings would take me. (My partner) the other butterfly suddenly dropped and reversed direction, heading underneath me (good one, partner!) I followed, rolling over and swooping across the water, low and fast. And then tragedy struck. I could see she was too low, I knew it was going to happen. The butterfly's wingtip brushed the water, upsetting the surface tension. The water sucked her down.

I sensed her cry out, I sensed her terror. Her feelings were so clear, so amplified, so terrible. I watched with dread. She's going to die, there's no help for a butterfly, floating in the river, colours all soaked, wings all wet.

The butterfly struggled, but it was no use, she would tear her wings off before becoming airborne. I felt tears sting my eyes. I was part of this tragedy. It was immediate, and real. There was nothing I could do about it, I thought, gliding over her struggling body as it drifted down the stream. We passed a human, standing in the river, his eyes closed. Might as well have been a statue. What good is that, I thought. He could have saved her!

With a jolt I brought my consciousness back to my body, looking out of my own eyes. I turned just in time to see the poor butterfly float past and around a bend a few metres downstream. I ran to catch her. The trees blocked my path, forcing me to duck and weave. I stubbed my toes on the rocks in the riverbed. And she floated, wings open to the sky, not struggling anymore, waiting for her saviour.

Eventually, the river widened and I managed to scoop her out of the water, set her down on a large, flat rock in the wan sunlight.

I tried to project my mind once again, to coax some thought from the limp body, but received neither glimmer of joy nor whisper of word. Maybe the cry of terror was especially intense, maybe that was why I had heard it, and I couldn't hear her thoughts later. Maybe butterflies have very little voices and are difficult to hear.

I waded up the river quietly, returning to my backpack and shoes. The light was beginning to fail, the sun having already set behind the western mountains. I wanted to be away from the dampness of the river-course before I settled down for the night. I quickly dried my feet with the outside of my socks, and pulled my boots on.

I had a vision of the butterfly, lying on the rock. The bright colours flowed out of her wings and rushed together in a fountain of light that burst out above the limp form on the rock to create a new fluid form. A deva, a spirit, a winged form of colour and light and consciousness. I had the feeling it smiled at me, then it shot off downstream.

Maybe I couldn't delay the inevitable. Her body had become a chrysalis for a second metamorphosis.

What was happening to me, I wondered. Was I going mad, or was I becoming more sane? Whether or not I'd heard a butterfly's thoughts, I felt wiser for having had a moment to appreciate their fleeting beauty and ultimate fragility.

\* \* \*

Supper was a can of baked beans with some biscuits. I tidied up the crumbs, and stowed the dirty can in my backpack. Tired and melancholy, I retired.

There were no stars that night, so it remained warm, the clouds acting like a blanket. I slept soundly in the lower boughs of a tree, waking partially to shift every hour or so as the stiffness crept in.

\* \* \*

When I looked down from my tree I discovered that my backpack was gone. Disappeared! I swung down from the branches, wincing as my stiffness made itself known. Sleeping in the tree had seemed like a good idea, safe from predators and creepy crawlies. But I had forgotten to take my pack up into the tree, and something had taken it. I cursed. My food, my waterbottle, my windbreaker jacket, gone! I searched the surrounding bush in all directions, looking for clues. I found some baboon droppings, and the empty, dented bean-can.

I gazed up at the peak I still wanted to climb. It loomed above me, outlined against the bright, pre-dawn sky. There was still a blanket of pale grey clouds, and an atmosphere of fantasy. My dragon would be roosting in a cave somewhere far above, lying on a pile of gold. Bronze Dragon Peak, I decided. Shouldn't take more than three hours to ascend, two to descend, and I could still be back at the car and my supplies by nightfall.

I scanned the contours for a route. There was an easy way through the southern foothills; a long, slow detour. Another route passed directly up the river-gullies and cliffs of the western face. It looked steep in places, but there didn't seem to be any impossible traverses. The steep western face then. Adventure, hardship, challenge and all that.

There was a vague path that wound up to the base of the cliffs, some four-hundred metres above the valley floor. Then the mountain rose steeply, in uneven steps, including a steep section of ridge that required some intelligent route planning. Up close, the cliffs looked a lot steeper than they had from the river. I pressed on, eager to gain the view from the peaks, to triumph high above.

The route became more and more challenging; it was not obvious where to climb. Fantastic rock formations jutted out from the cliffs, red-brown and pale orange, blocking my progress. I slowed down, planning each short ascent, each traverse carefully. Right hand here, left hand there, left foot there .. no, that didn't work, I couldn't reach it .. left foot there, right foot next to it .. stretch, climb, pause .. stretch, pull, pause ..

My adrenaline was flowing, focusing my mind, eliminating all superfluous thought, channelling all my attention into the act of climbing. The cliffs became steeper, pushing me out into the air. I felt lean and strong, hungry. I was in command of my body, command of the rockface.

Stretch, pull, pause .. stretch, climb, pause.

[Finally you make silence]

The eagle's greeting filled my empty mind. Just in time, I

remembered to lift up and away from the thoughts that were stirring in the pool of my mind.

I focused on one simple thought, and projected it toward the eagle, wherever it was. "Hello, my flying friend," I thought. I craned my neck backwards, but it was a position I couldn't safely maintain. I paused in my climbing, listening calmly.

[storms come / dark sky]

My mind provided the words, as a translation of the images. I looked out to the western horizon. The clouds were lower than they had been in the morning, and had darkened somewhat. Still, they looked harmless enough. It might rain, but only late that evening.

"Thank you, I'll watch it," I responded, thinking the warning a little premature. I was glad to be able to finally communicate without drowning the eagle in the stormy sea of my mind.

"How do you achieve silence?" I asked.

[as you do / think of one moment]

I realised that I was doing that because I was on the rock, climbing. I was immersed in the challenge, thinking of the present moment only. Normally I would think of the past and the future as well, with worries, memories, regrets, fears, hopes and expectations all creating their own dialogues. A mere shadow of the past and future existed in the present, yet my mind always dwelled on them.

"Adding substance to shadow, adding substance ever more," I sang quietly to myself, Rodriguez lyrics that had new meaning.

[what you see inside you see outside] the eagle agreed.

[why do you not fly?]

"I don't have my wings," I explained.

[don't need wings to fly] he replied.

Flying without wings? That would be impossible.

[Impossible is something that can't be done / something you believe can't be done?]

I turned this thought slowly over and over in my mind, appreciating the distinction.

[Watch this]

I turned and caught a flash of black feathers streaking across the sky. The eagle was close, level with me, outlined against the horizon. His wings were tucked in, I could see his neckfeathers quivering with the speed as he hurtled by. His body was jet black, with a thin white band on his midriff. He spread his wings suddenly, and climbed upwards, rode into the sky, and ...

Vanished!

I looked everywhere for a sign of where he could have gone. There were no black spots in the distant cloud that could have hid his outline. There was nothing nearby, he had been high up, in open air, and I still had an unobstructed view of where he should have been.

Nothing! Gone, gone, gone.

That could not have happened. It was illogical. It was impossible!

Which just proved his point. There was possible a larger reality than I could understand. If my world was built out of things I believed were possible, maybe it was time I began to expand my expectations.

The eagle was still gone, so after waiting for a while, I returned to my climbing. The cliffs eased off, the slope became more gentle, and then there was only one large boulder to be climbed and I was standing on the summit. Bronze Dragon Peak.

I spread my arms and pretended to soar in the wind that blew up the slope I had just conquered. I breathed in the intoxicating fresh air that rewards every climber at his goal.

The noon sun was a white disc of light that filtered down over the dim lands, colouring the high points with cold-steel silver. The wind had strengthened rapidly. It was now a gusty howl that chilled me through my shirt and jeans. I pulled on a cotton sweater, my last item of clothing, and squatted down in the protected lee of a boulder.

The clouds were rolling a dark grey canopy in from the west now, alarmingly low, pregnant with rain. There was no time to indulge in the satisfaction of being on the summit. The dark dragon was about to come home to roost on the mountain. I began to wonder if I had not miscalculated the remaining time to escape.

I looked down the slope, then back to the clouds. If I scrambled down the mountain, I could be down the slope and back on the path to the western mountains by the time the rain hit. I would get wet, but I would reach the car that evening and be able to change into dry clothes. And there was food in the car! My stomach growled. I could do with some food - I was beginning to feel light-headed.

I scrambled, but going down a cliff face is even slower than going up. I had not made even half-way down the cliffs before a few drops spattered out of the sky in warning, and I looked out into the valley in dread. The cloud was dumping water, drenching the ground, the bushes, the rocks, sluicing down in sheets that hid the valley from view. I couldn't continue, I was approaching the worst part of the cliffs. With no visibility and slippery, wet rocks, I did not rate my chances of survival.

I found a cave. It was small, but it was deep enough to be dry.

The rain drummed into the dust at the mouth of the cave. It came faster and faster, pounding with a rolling beat, then a steaming hiss, finally a roar. I shrank back against the cold rocks, trying to avoid the fine spray that was drifting in. I hugged my knees to my chest. This might be the beginning of the cold front. If I did not find a break between this cloud and the next, I could be holed up there for ages. I shuddered.

There had to be a break in the clouds. The first cloud, the dark dragon, had been way out in front, all by itself. Hadn't it?

There was no break in the clouds.

It rained.

# TOUCH OF THE SPIRIT

Cold. Coldcoldcold. I woke again. I was huddled against the rocks, my legs shivering uncontrollably. It was too cold to sleep.

Every half-hour I had to stand up, force the blood to circulate in my legs. Drop for twenty press-ups, up for twenty jumps. Ow! I cracked my hand against the roof of the cave. Running on the spot, punching the air. Slowly some warmth returned. Then I huddled down on the floor, dropping my head onto my knees again, trying in vain to sleep. I felt small, alone, and frail.

I tried to conserve my energy, holding my body calm, keeping my warmth contained. I visualised flames surrounding my body. It didn't work very well. I spent most of the night staring into the dark, expecting my clothes to burst into flame, yet feeling cold.

The slow agonising hours of the graveyard shift came and went. I waited, shivering, thinking of my great hunger and how I had no supplies at all. The rain pounded down outside the cave.

Dawn was no great event, it just became less dark, then grey. Then - nothing. It rained, it was cold. The water puddled at the mouth of the cave and ran inside, leaving me with only a narrow strip of dry dust and hard rock. I was tired, I ached deep in my bones. Because I was hungry I could not fend off the cold very well. There was plenty of water, though. I cupped my hands at the mouth of the cave and drank from the runoff.

I wondered if I was destined to become a skeleton, up there in the dragon's lair. I had all the time in the world to think about my life, and what I was doing with it. Raindrops pattered softly, monotonously, onto the cave floor. I stared out into the greyness. I slowed my breathing to a gentle rise and fall. I would meditate, I decided, and see how deep I could go.

I shifted to sit cross-legged and eased my back against the wall. I began to sink down into my being, observing the thoughts that drifted by. Deeper and darker, a silent space that expanded into vastness. My attention sank like a diving probe in an abyss. No sound, no light, no thought, only ... blackness.

Suddenly I was face to face with a terrifying mask of cracking, translucent skin stretched over an alabaster skull. The creature's face changed, it shivered to form a gnarled spider's head, mandibles curling hungrily. Shiver. An orcish beast with huge, rotting tusks. Shiver. A deathly black, giant panther with glowing red eyes. Then the guardian settled into a tall skeleton, black cape clinging to his angular form, his cowled skull dark. His eyes were empty sockets like gateways to a cold and empty universe. He laughed, a humourless sound, like rocks tumbling down an endless cliff.

"And so we finally meet, fugitive," he said. He spoke in a way that made my eardrums vibrate. It was as if the guardian had taken form. I could feel the pressure of his presence in the cave. "Inside you there is a dead man, waiting to get out," he said in that chilling voice. I could feel my skeleton respond to his call, vibrating with a weirdly hollow resonance.

I wanted to run away, to escape.

"There is nowhere to go now." Death looked through me. "Everyone meets me in the end." He lifted a skull in his skeletal hand, and crushed it to dust with a sickening crunch. He let the dust tip into the dark wind.

"You know I am here, but you pretend I am not. You think you can escape my grasp. You ignore your fears and tempt the fate beyond. I shall take you, for you are too reckless. You have pushed too far. You will die here. You fool."

"I c-c-can just open my eyes and walk away," I stuttered, determined to hold my own.

Death laughed hollowly, and waved his hand "Try it."

He moved in an instant, he stood now at my side with one skeletal hand gripping the hair at the base of my skull. "Try," he repeated, mocking me.

I was beginning to panic. This meditation was weird and frightening and all too real. I forced myself to open my eyes, to snap out of the altered state.

Nothing happened. I opened my eyes to Death's grin, his foul breath was staining my skin grey. I screamed. I was awake, fully conscious and yet somewhere in the bowels of hell.

"You have pushed too far," Death repeated, "there is no return from here." He chuckled like a scattering of pebbles. I began to run, stumbling in the darkness, but there was nowhere to run to, I was in a place of blackness, and Death held me tight.

"What do you want from me?" I shouted at Death, though he was beside me.

"Your life. We must wait until your body has passed away from hunger, then I shall come to collect your soul. Just be patient. You will learn to be patient." He roared with laughter, and my bones vibrated.

Blood pounded in my ears. I crouched down, hugging my knees. I felt so small. But then I had an idea. "What if you are just a limitation, a fear, like all the others?" I asked.

Death looked slightly put out, as if I had called him Jimmy, instead of Lord Death. He pressed his alabaster face against mine. I smelled attar and damp bone. A cold rage was building within his cloak, and whispers of frozen air escaped from the folds. He grew in size, pushing me backwards.

"I am DEATH," he breathed, his foul blackness enveloping me.

"You are just a fear!" I shouted. Light filled the emptiness, bursting through his cloak, spilling into his eye sockets. "You exist only when I believe you are the End! There is no end, the spirit is indestructible, and I live!"

The guardian of death vanished. There was a gulf before me, a chasm that separated me from another plane, but I could not see what lay ahead. I tried to step through the transition, to take myself into the beyond.

A bright being stood before me, a transparent form with wide wings, her hand held up to forestall me. An angel.

*To live forever, you have to let go of who you are.*

Who was I?

I saw myself as I was, a free spirit, yet connected through love to my family and friends, burdened by some guilts, governed by my principles, my philosophies. The striving for perfection. The imperative of honesty. Pacifism. Rejection of materialism. My many personal rules that structured me as I was.

Like weeds, clinging to my feet, rooting me to the soil of my reality. They prevented me from changing, from really being free. Not all of who I was was necessary. I could leave some aspects behind. But what of those aspects that I wanted to keep?

*You leave behind who you are. All of it, good and bad.*

I could end up being anybody after that. Absolutely anybody. I could be somebody I wouldn't have liked before. An aggressive wife-beater. Or a thief. Or worse. Tinker, tailor, soldier, sailor .. went the nursery rhyme. Rich man, poor man, beggar man, thief.

Then again, if I left who I was behind, I would be capable of choosing anything. There would be no rules to limit me.

The idea was exciting. The possibilities! I could be whoever I wanted to be. The only thing that kept me being who I was were the weeds that I used for stability and comfort. Hah! I could cut free, and change.

I had a sudden fear. Who would I be? How would I ever know who the real me was? Shifting and changing, shifting and changing, forever lost in the endless patterns of the world.

The angel came close.

*That fear causes you to keep an identity, to mold an ego. It pulls your spirit away from change. The fear is unnecessary. Spirit is indestructable. It is always learning, no matter what identity you take on, what role you play.*

I examined myself, observing every weed that rooted me to my identity, and slowly, one by one, cut them free. Some were easy to remove, the leftovers of obsolete character traits. Others had become part of my flesh, part of my belief of who and what I was, and these were harder to leave behind. But finally I was free, just a single idea of life.

I stepped across the gulf, past the angel, into the beyond.

The world was filled with light, but there was more than just light, there was a concentration of distilled consciousness that was everywhere. I didn't dare to breathe in case I disturbed the vision. I soaked up the elation. It felt like love, but so intense it thickened the air. It surrounded me, penetrated me.

I absorbed the light, and so became enlightened. It couldn't be learned, I realised, it had to be tapped into. I felt fuller, wiser. What could I become if I stayed here? I wondered.

But I could not maintain the awareness any longer than a few moments, it was too intense, too rich. I tried to hold on, to draw more from that precious state, but I was pushed outwards and away. My perceptions began to cloud. I could barely see the light but I knew that it was there, knew that I had been a part of it. Strands of light slipped through my clutching fingers like soft strips of silk, slipping like vapours now, just a trace remaining .. gone! without a sound.

The sand was wet and stuck to my fingers when I tried to brush them clean. I was lying on my stomach on the ground, my head resting on my arm, my left leg bent. I had no idea how long I had been lying there, but it was dark. I rose and stepped out of the cave.

I was changed. I felt weightless, and at peace.

I stood on the high slopes of the mountains, raised above the darkened land, lifted into the sky. The air was icy, fresh from the rains, and crystal clear. There was not a breath of wind. Into this silent theatre, the stars had entered from the deepness of space, sparkling their brilliant light in the collective patterns of constellations. A silver haze hinted at distant galaxies. Orion dipped towards the western horizon, retiring below the dramatic curve of the Milky Way. The Southern Cross stood out strongly, and the two pointer stars shone with crystal clarity. There were stars, more and more stars, filling the sky in awesome patterns, painting the night with breathtaking beauty.

There was balance and harmony in my heart. That great starscape out beyond the earth was somehow inside me as well. It felt as if I had swallowed a universe of my own.

# FIELDS OF GOLD

It seemed that she asked me, "Why do you cry so in the morning sunlight. Why do tears fall from your face like rain from wetted leaves? What is it that pains you so?" I could only paint her thoughts with my interpretation, for everything came to me as poetry, through a fugue. She seemed too far away, a ghost in the brightness of day, this woman before me. Kim from the city. Kim from the past.

I cried not from pain but from joy, because I saw beauty in the waking day, and the fiery sun lit up my heart, illuminating a silent knowledge. I was inspired by the words of Creation written into the fabric of all that was around me. The browns of the rocks in shadow, the golds of the rocks in sun, the sinuous trace of movement made by a passing bird, the edge of the sky that ran along the mountainous horizon.

She touched my arm, she comforted me, her dark hair soft about her lovely face. Her eyes fell upon my desperate body, she looked with fear at my ribs, my chest heaving, my body thinned after the hunger of days, walking through the hills of my awakening, running through the wilderness of the lands I had returned through. But my hunger didn't matter, it was of no concern to me. For I had emerged on the other side of it into the glorious morning, this rich soliloquy of elements and colour. The tears rolled down my face.

She wanted to hold me, to protect me from myself, and her arms wrapped around me, I was curled in her arms, as the sun showered upon my heart, filling me with joy, it filled me but it only warmed her back, she didn't notice how the sun passed into me through her encircling arms.

She smelled me, the sweat of days on me, from the strain of surviving, the dirt beaten into my sun-burned skin over the hills and valleys and the peaks, and I must have smelled as strong as the cattle on the plains. I could only smell the energy of life exuding from my pores, I was in a plane so different from the heavy scents of sweat and dust that filled her nostrils and yet I was before her, seeming to be in her world. She hugged me closer, though it was hard for her to do so. So determined in her gentle ways she was.

She wrapped me in her soft flesh and for a brief moment I wished that I smelt washed, like her. So that I would be the same, so that she could understand me, have some affect on me. And the sun shone through her like water falling through a sieve.

I turned my face up to the sky, the mass of all colours blue, dissolved in amongst each other in thick swirls that I could taste, a sweet mixture of the vanished and the invisible. And I breathed in a shuddering draught of it, that I might eat from the very sky above me. The weight of the sky pressed into my body, filled me with its empty essence.

I watched a fearless eagle soar and wheel high above the plains, falling into a dive, arcing back into the heights, wings spread wide. I could see the wind rushing through his feathers, the strain of the carving turns pulled across my chest, and from my beak came the defiant cry of freedom.

"Will you stay with me, will you be my love?" she asked, stretching out her hand to keep me on the earth, yearning to have me by her side, to live and share and work and pass away, another human life spent in the safety and comfort too far beneath the sun to ever reach it.

I kissed her then, pushed her away as I kissed her, threw my body away from her grasp, and yet I recognised her face, the familiar curves of her subtle body, I knew her from a life gone by, before the days in the mountains, a life when I could still love her as she needed to be loved. Yet I loved her still, but in no way the same as that love of before. For I was free.

The kisses and the passion were a part of her world, I could not take them and remain in the plane that I was in. I loved her as I loved the wind, the coolness of the morning dew, the rainbow in a waterfall. Because she was alive I loved her, I was linked to it all with love, pouring through me in a flood that would surely have burst my heart, before.

Kim, dear Kimberley May, had driven out from the city, all the way out to the Cedarberg, to find me. She knew this was where I would be, knew from the tales I had told on those long nights beside the fire, curled in comfort and security. She had found me as I returned to Porterville, heading for food.

"Goodbye my lover, goodbye my friend," I called out. "I can't stay with you, but I may see you in the end."

I ran out across the fields, the gold of the wheatfields striking my legs and exploding in an irregular rhythm of dusty seeds, I ran over the dark stones and they felt soft and yielding, and the ground became the black of space, although it was rock, look how it cut into my bare feet, but it was space as well, the vast open heavens and the golden seeds were the stars, and I ran from one galaxy of seeds to the next, swirling a trail of comets behind me, stars clinging to my sweating limbs, sticking into my hair in a mane of planets and suns, swinging about my shoulders in cosmic splendour.

I glanced back across the waving wheat, across the field to where she stood, white dress blowing in the gentle wind, standing in the middle of her own universe of stars, although she could not see them. About her legs the stars brushed each other, the suns and planets swirled within reach, all she had to do was bend down and sweep her hand through that energy, to create her own reality, to liberate her life.

But she could not see the power around her, she was blinded by the sun, gravity pressed her into the hard earth, the world she saw was not my world, and her reality held her captive. She stretched her hand out to me, reaching for a dream she could never own. She did not try to follow, she was too rooted to her place. She cried softly, then whirled in anger, and moved like a storm, to the road, back to her motorcar, beyond the slamming door and screeching tyres, back from whence she had come.

I could show her nothing, for she would not see me, she would always see something else. If I joined her, I would become only a reflection of her expectations, a creation of her need. Her error was in trying to possess me.

You have not lost anything, my love, for I never did belong to you. Nor you to me. I have claimed freedom for my own. When you claim that same freedom, you shall discover that I never ran away from you across the fields of gold, out into the dusty plains under this blessed sky. I ran towards you, towards the enlightened spirit of your future. There will come a moment when we shall embrace again, and I will be closer to you than I could ever have been before.

Until that time, it will seem that I am farther away from you than the stars.

She had vanished from my world again.

I was left with the wind.

I loved the wind.

# DREAMWEAVER

I work through the firehot day
to create a sculptured form of beauty
at last it is complete, perfected on a stand
I leave the room to eat my evening meal
but alas! my careless mind and hand
knock it from the rest; it falls
and smashes tiny fragments on the floor
smashes tiny fragments
tiny on the floor

A snarl of anger curls my lips
and I howl my rage at beauty lost
so careless in my hunger, distracted
I destroyed my work of days gone by
I sigh a resolution to re-create
and fall upon my tired bed
fall upon my
fall

I sink gently into the softness
of warm, quiet dissolve'd sleep
images float idly upward
in the liquid imagination I have become
and a smile
ripples through my languid body
a smile ripples
a smile

A familiar landscape rises
through the silver liquid of my dream
the mountains sharp in ridge and rock
the plains so soft in moist repose
I am the sun
drenching lands red and molten gold
I am the sun
I am

The currents in the tide of air
wisp and spin amidst my laze
I wash against the browns of earth
and wish to fuel the rising air
below the curve of my outstretched arms
then I could fly all night all day
then I could fly
I fly

I fly so free an eagle form
beneath tall clouds and sparkling sky
but suddenly I recall
how my trailing, careless hand did knock
that sculptured beauty from my life
and anger splits my sky
with lightning white
thunder splits my sky
thunder white

I rise gently into the freshness
of warm and vibrant solid day
memories sink idly downward
forgotten amid the rumpled sheets
but a smile
defines my crystal body
a smile defines
a smile

A familiar landscape rises
through the certain passage of my day
the mountains sharp in ridge and rock
the plains so soft in moist repose
And I see the sun
drenching lands red and molten gold
I see the sun
I see

The currents in the tide of air
wisp and spin o'er morning's laze
and wash against the browns of earth
I hope this fuels the rising air
below the curve of my outstretched wings
then I can fly all day all night
then I can fly
I fly

I fly so free a glider form
beneath tall clouds and sparkling sky
but suddenly I recall
how in my dream the thunder roared
I spiral down to safer ground
as angry sky explodes
in dark and might
the sky explodes
the angry sky

Could it be that Yesterday
Shattered by my careless hand
became the pattern for a conscious dream
and with symbolic power
created the form of my Tomorrow
forging anger into a thundershower
anger forged
a thundershower

\* \* \*

When I dreamt of the eagles, of their black wings outlined against
the brilliant white of curling clouds, bodies flying in loose formation
with me, spiralling slowly into the cloud, I knew that I would meet
them soon in the more solid light of day. When I stood ready, I stilled
my thoughts, found the quiet centre of my internal universe, the axis
of all the stars. I projected a clear greeting to the eagles in the sky.
They were silent, but I knew that I would find them, that it was time.

My glider tugged at my harness, then boosted me up and away as
the wind caught the gossamer sail. The air rushed past my body, a cool
current that whistled through my lines. In no time at all, I was circling
high above the mountain, the world spread out at my feet in majestic
splendour. A large cloud beckoned from above, and I glided over to
its lifting currents, climbing through a hazy inversion layer, higher
and higher into the cold, crisp clarity near the cumulus. Then the air
became misty, pregnant with water-vapour, condensing, collecting
in shrouds and wisps, thickening and wrapping me in wetness. The
ground disappeared, the sky disappeared, and I entered the swirling
quiet place where rain is created.

I recognised everything. I had been here before, and yet, this was
new. I looked up to my wing, and saw three eagles, banked in harmony
with me, arcing in a loose formation through the grey and viscous air.
We were isolated in a tiny world, just the four of us. In the pearly
light, I could see no further than the highest eagle, and I watched
closely to maintain the formation, holding a steady turn. If any one of
us broke the formation, we would never find each other again.

[Hail, Eaglefriend] came the thought, precise and clear.

"Hello, my eagles." I swelled with happiness.

[you have achieved much since I last saw you] said the highest
eagle, her mental presence familiar to me.

I blinked the water-droplets out of my eyes. That high eagle had some distinctive markings.

"Sundancer! Hello, you beauty. Where have you been flying?"

[the far side of death]

She wasn't there now, was she? I wasn't dead, or dreaming. It was hard to tell, my world had become a shifting fluid experience.

"How do I see you now?" I asked.

[I can come here, as I will. You are closer to my plane too]

"I died, in consciousness, and rose reborn," I explained.

We circled in silence for a minute, just appreciating the company.

[you still haven't worked it out] Sundancer said softly.

"?" I asked, striving to improve the brevity of my thoughts.

The darkest of the eagles drifted closer to me, coming in to within a metre. He was jet black, with a white band on his midriff. His wings were deep and broad, his black leading-edge feathers were glossy. He peered at me with intensely.

[your friend] said Sundancer.

I remembered music, notes tumbling over each other. I remembered a mountain peak, a cliff face, a body lying at its base, broken, legs twisted, blood staining a dark shirt. I remembered Beagle, and the jarring impact as an eagle slammed into his body, at the end. I recognised that striking eagle now. She was gliding above my wing.

"Why?" I cried up to Sundancer. "Why did he have to die?"

[He chose it so. But he began to fear. I reminded him to let go.]

I was numbed. The very second I should have seen was the one instant I had blocked in my mind. Beagle had triumphed over death, not failed. The eagle had not sealed his fate, she had been his saviour.

"Why did he choose to die?"

[to show his friend the way]

"He died for my enlightenment?" I was incredulous.

[In a way. You chose fear, and missed the learning, until now]

"How could he sacrifice his life?"

[He wanted to initiate his own transition. Nobody really dies] Sundancer reminded me.

"So where did he go? What has become of him?" I was too eager, bubbling with questions.

I was met with silence. I knew I should have reigned in my thoughts more severely. I found my focus again.

"Well?" I asked.

The black-eagle male drifted in closer to me. He stared at me through one light-brown eye. The big black eagle with a white cord-marking around its midriff.

[Do I look the part?] he asked.

I stared. I was speechless.

[Always be prepared!] he cried. His motto. Then he rolled and carved away. I banked my glider hard over to the right, chasing him. The remaining two eagles broke formation then, and I lost sight of them. I was intent only on catching Beagle, the rapscallion, the rogue; my friend. He weaved and rolled and tumbled and looped. At last he vanished into the grey secret of the cloud, beyond the range of my clumsy lunges.

[Do not believe only that which you see, or you'll see only that which you believe] he chided me,

"So you are still here, you joker! I thought you'd have disappeared."

Laughter. [Of course I'm still here, circling the Earth], he replied. [Few can pass from our plane to perfection in one leap. I have shifted up. There is a great journey ahead. One step up on the stairway to heaven.] He laughed again, and came diving out of the grey cloud past my head.

"Life doesn't cease when you die?" I asked.

[You just learn how to climb higher mountains] he answered.

He scribed a wide arc in the air before me.

[I leave to rejoin Sundancer. Fly! And believe!]

The grey cloud swallowed his form. The smile remained on my face. I glided on, until I burst out of the cloud high above the ground.

The view was breathtaking. The tumbling white wall of cloud dropped down below me in the dazzling sunlight. It towered above me as well, rising another thousand metres into the deep blue sky. The wind was icy, and I was soaking wet, yet I didn't notice the cold, I was too inspired to feel cold.

Below me, spread out in grandeur, was the Earth. Mountains, softened by the altitude, melted into the plains in swathes of dark rock. The fields linked together in a patchwork fantasy of greens and golds, siennas and ochre, cinnamon and pastel jade, white sand and black quarry-rock. A herd of animals moved as a concert of dots across dusty brown camps. Farmsteads provided tiny points of focus for other tiny buildings to cluster around, each huddle another farm, each farm a sphere of nurturing human attention, urging the ground to yield life to the world. The earth pulsed with a deep vitality. And from the high mountain peaks, rivers flowed with the nectar of life. Trees sheltered in the winding river-courses, offering protection to their own kind. I looked down at my home, and marvelled at the beauty of it.

I reached out my hand, and waved a magical pass over the land.

The beauty, the breathtaking mystery and inspiring creation vanished and became a dull opacity. Below me was just the ground, just scenery, an arbitrary collection of structures and animals and people that had no meaning.

I reached out my hand again, and welcomed back the magic of my dreams. It was a new landscape, a new land, pulsing with vitality and awareness.

Nothing had changed.

An eagle cried its defiant power in a shout of triumph.

I cried out with it.

Everything had changed.

# THE SUN SHINES!

*It was a sky*
*filled with rising promise*
*a day*
*of tumultuous adventure*
*Perspective exploded*
*outwards into my mind*
*leaving the earth behind*
*in an everyday haze*
*how we forget*
*and how we remember!*
*the Sun shines eternal*
*if we can fly high enough.*

# ABOUT THE AUTHOR

After writing this book, I embarked on a quest to create a great big fantasy saga. This became The Tale of the Lifesong, an epic fantasy set in an older world, where magic was still a raw force.

It has absolutely nothing to do with paragliding, but if you want a fast-and-furious story with a mystic twist, then by all means check out what I've been up to on greghamerton.com.

And of course I'm still flying! Ten years after writing Beyond The Invisible, I decided to make a short film about that special freedom you can find in the sky. You can watch a sample on eternitypress.com.

Enjoy your adventures, wherever your dreams take you ...

*Greg Hamerton*

CPSIA information can be obtained
at www.ICGtesting.com
Printed in the USA
BVHW020108090123
655872BV00024B/192